# SEXY TEASERS

*Lesbian Erotica*

Faye Love

*I would like to thank my love, who has guided and helped me through the process of writing and publishing this book.*
*I would also love to thank my dear friend and benefactor. I'm not sure which of us are more insane, but I truly appreciate you and your belief in me. Thank you with all that I have and am.*
*Thanks to the kind and sexy Lesbians at Alter Egos Publishing and the editing team for taking me on and taking the chance. Not seeming to mind my terrible spelling errors and sometimes chaotic organization skills. I truly appreciate you and am proud to be a part of your rising rainbow writing team.*
*Thanks to all the Lesbians out there who read, explore, and dream. Whose imaginations run wild either in the light, or in the dark. Thank you for contributing to my creativity. May these stories cause you intense pleasure, and unquenchable frustration.*

*Thank you, Faye Love*

# CONTENTS

Chapter 1

# Bookstore-Part 1

Singing to the song R.E.S.P.E.C.T, I walked down the street with a certain pep in my step. My golden locks swayed in beat as I sashayed down the street like a runway model. I could very well be that. With my deep dark gray eyes, petite frame and 5'6 height, I could kill it! This time of day everyone is still in bed, snuggling close to someone. Which I am currently not doing, because men tend to be assholes. I'm not gonna let thoughts of my obnoxious ex bring me down though. I refuse to allow him to kill my light. Smiling brightly, I looked at the rising sun. Been one whole month without the cheating creep. Which means six whole weeks without sex. Don't get me wrong, him and I had a very healthy sex life... That is, until he got himself fired. So, I put him on a two-week probation. Then the ass went out and slept around. I caught him on the night we were supposed to have make up sex. I'm really disliking men right about now! Every time I give them a chance, they mess it up. I know not all of them are bad, but one rotten apple generally spoils the bunch. And I'm getting really tired of biting into rot.

This early in the morning there's not much open, so imagine my shock when I saw an open sign at one of the local bookstores. It was a simple brick building with a name that read 'Impulse Bookstore'. Shrugging my shoulders, I walked in. Might as well find something to occupy my new free time. It was like any other bookstore. Walls lined with shelves of books. Dark wood tables next to comfy looking couches. There was no one at the front desk so I walked down the aisles lightly gliding my fingertips on the newly bound books. Lost in thought, I wandered down row after row. Some titles catching my attention. I pulled a few books from the shelves, collecting them in my arms when I heard a faint noise of what seemed like a whimper. Following the noise, I discovered that I was close to the back of the store. The sounds led me to a beautiful mahogany door, closed.

A short internal battle raged within me while I determined if I should or shouldn't investigate the noise. It could be something bad, like a killer, and if so, then I am doing what every white girl in the history of movies has ever done. But what if an old lady who probably owns this place fell and broke her hip? I can't just leave; she could be hurt! I took a deep breath and opened the door. Needless to say, what I saw was not what I was expecting.

Sitting in a leather chair, a woman had her head back, legs opened, exposing herself to me. Tattoos decorated her smooth legs, that draped over each arm of the chair. Pants, shoes, and underwear were tossed to the floor. And two, long fingers were knuckles deep into her clearly soaked opening. I was mesmerized. Her deep moans of pleasure shook me to the center of my soul as her fingers pumped steadily in and out of her with a growing speed. Never have I been so turned on by another women. Her liquid shined as it flowed onto the cushion under her. I could feel my own arousal instantly growing at the sight of her. My body heating up at the desire now posed. Her naked body glistening with sweat, as her clean sweet aroma filled the room. I bit my lip in anticipation as my core twitched and heart rate increased.

She began to rock her hips and roughly twist and pinch her pink nipples, moaning louder now. Her flower opened before me, as she penetrated herself. Slick essences illuminated the dark pink of her inner lips. Her muscles contracting as her orgasm neared. They bulged, like that of a hard worker, flexing and relaxing with each movement. What the? Who the hell has those kinds of muscles working at a bookstore? What the fuck kind of person has that? Her body shook as she squirted all over her hand, screaming out her pleasure. Hell, I was sexually frustrated and here before me is sex on a freaking platter! I couldn't help the moan that escaped my lips. Or the loud crash of the books falling from my weakening arms.

I jumped back at the loud noise, and she... She froze. Oh no. Shit I'm in for it now! Her head rose up as black curls framed her almost angelic face. Her beauty alone captured me. She has to be the most enticing, beautiful, exotic woman I have ever seen. Her eyes a rebellious dark blue that stilled me where I stood. Her pink lips swollen with the force of her bite. Her steady eyes widened in shock, but still fogged with lust. I need to change my panties; I need to change my mind. Fuck, I need to change my seemingly infinite lack of control... like right now.

"How did you get in here?" Her voice was deep with lust, raspy as if she'd just woken up. Her accent was strange, as if she were from the Ukraine. But that did little to hinder the sexiness of her voice. Her eyes slowly traveled up my body as she spoke. Her fingers still buried within her. I couldn't speak, could hardly move. Could barely breathe. I was freaking petrified, as she silently waited for my response. My eyes were glued to her. As her hips slowly rocked on her fingers. Her eyes holding me steady. Seeing that I was unable to respond and seemed to resemble a deer in headlights instead of a functional human being, she continued to further raise my stress level as she slid her hand slowly out of her slick opening. Her smooth long fingers were glistening with her juices. To my purest of shock, she brought her fingers to her mouth and sensually licked her essence clean off each finger. Putting on a porn like show. By now I am certain that the crotch of my pants has a noticeable wet spot. Slowly she stood up, swaying her hips as she approached me. Her white, button down shirt falling, just below her once exposed slit. She stood like a vision of beauty in a dream of horror. Thick eyelashes, red lips, dreamy muscles, and incredibly tall. She is the tallest woman that I've ever seen. Her hair fell around her like a curly black blanket. Reaching all the way down to her lower back. She could be a model, an Amazon, something unreal.

"Would you like to participate?" She slowly licked her lips, my eyes unable to look away as she edged closer. "I could please you more than you've ever been before. I could awaken your deepest primal urges, sweet girl." As if by divine intervention, I was snapped from my trance. She's a Witch! A deadly, beautiful witch! She continued her slow approach and before she could say anything else and put me back under her hypnotic spell, I turned tail and ran.

⊠

Chapter 2

# Bookstore-Part 2

To say I was avoiding that bookstore like it was the Black Death was an understatement. It's been over a month and I refuse to even drive down that street now. At night when I'm in bed, it's all I can think about. Her, that woman, the image of her gyrating on her fingers, overtook my actions. I was unaware that my hand had traveled down into my pants and started rubbing, thinking of her dark blue eyes, and relentless moans until...

"Aunty Em, what are you doing?" Jumping up I clutched my chest as my heart raged. What the fuck? When did he get here? Quickly removing my hand and cursing myself, for clearly not paying attention, I smiled.

"Nothing sweetie, Aunty had an itch." Nodding his head, he looked around taking everything in. He's a very smart kid. He then looked me up and down, shaking his head.

"Are you wearing that?" Looking down I looked at my light blue faded skinny jeans and dark blue tank top. I looked ok. "Wearing this to what and what's wrong with what I'm wearing?" Smiling sheepishly at me he tilted his head to the side.

"Dad's book signing and release is today. Remember?" Dang it! That's today! Running into my room I threw on a dark gray silk blouse tucked into a tight skirt that stopped a little pass mid-thigh. Running my fingers through my hair I walked back into the living-room. Putting on matching dark gray heels. I hadn't even noticed my nephew was wearing a little suit. He's so cute! And I told him so, which made him blush.

"So, where's this thing at again?" I asked as I grabbed my purse and car keys. "Aunty, really?... The Bookstore. Book signing. Bookstore." Damn! Trying to keep from hyperventilating I took deep breaths. There's plenty of bookstores in this area. What are the odds? "O-oh, ok. Y-you better get home..."

"No, Aunty I want to ride with you." He followed me to the door. God, I hope it's any other store...

Sooo, no, no it wasn't. It was the same store that I've been intentionally avoiding. The good-sized bookstore was packed to the brim with excited readers. I never realized just how entirely boring this is! I love reading and information just as well as the next girl. But all they're talking about is the crap books my brother writes... Not that it's truly bad but oh my God! How can they not be tired of this, it's predictable, its already happened, it's nothing new. And frankly, though worded right, it's kind of pointless. Oh the fucking joy! Sitting back in a chair I closed my eyes. I'm so done. I just want to leave. It's been hours of nonstop talk about books. BOOKS!! And not just any books. But the same damn book! Groaning, I gently rubbed my temples.

"Em? Em!" Opening my eyes, I looked at my brother. "huh?" He, like me had gray eyes. But his hair was more a dirty blonde. His nose sharp, and he sported a styled short beard.

"I want you to meet someone. Em, this is Mesa, the Bookstore owner. Mesa this in my little sister Emma." Shifting my eyes from him, I looked at Mesa and almost died. It was her. And she was sexy. She was wearing a tight black leather dress with spiked heels and a wicked smile. Her already sharp blue eyes, even sharper. Half of her black curls were pinned up in an elegant bun with a few ringlets falling down on the sides, and the rest cascading down her back. She stood taller than my brother by a few inches. She's so big, like a super model. Hell, she puts me to shame.

Seeing my shocked expression, she smiled and took a step closer to me. Taking my hand in hers. Her grip was strong, her hands warming my entire body. Causing a blush to rise and my skin to tingle. Yup, still sitting down, I am now cornered. "What a pleasure it is seeing you again Emma Rose. We talked so briefly before, but your brother has told me much about you." He did what! Seductively she leaned in. Giving me full view of the swells of her breast. Oh my. My mouth ran dry, as my panties slowly grew wet. I feel betrayed, the idiot, telling this witch about me. Why doesn't he just hand me over on a silver platter, it'd be more convenient.

Trying not to breathe in her sweet smell of things I couldn't begin to describe; I gulped looking away nervously. Her thumb caressed the back of my hand. I glanced back at her, her eyes bore into my soul, locking me in their grasp. I found myself leaning towards her, almost unable to stop, almost not wanting to. I was getting closer to her red lips, her blue eyes that reminded me of dark waters, sinking into the unknown. Her smell drifted to me, filling my lungs and stealing my air Everything faded away but her. Her. I could hear my heartbeat. Feel the blood rush in my veins. Forgetting about my brother who was watching. Everything fell away, except her. Breathing was hard, focusing on anything but her was impossible. She had a look in her eyes. Like a cat does once it's cornered it prey, a smile of victory on her full lips. So close, I could almost touch them.

Someone called her name, and she let go of my hand, releasing me from her enticing clutches. The air rushed to my lungs as if I hadn't been breathing the entire time. She stood straight, winked at me, as if this incredibly odd encounter was not at all out of the norm. Then walked away, swaying her hips as she did so. No, something is not right with her! Not right with this! What the fuck just happened?

I jumped out of my seat and ran out the doors. Starving for air that didn't carry her scent. Why is she even more beautiful the second time around? Sweating, I leaned against the brick wall, looking up at the dark sky. Like her eyes, I felt myself falling up, into the unknown. And it's terrifying... After several deep breaths and calming exercises of logic, I eventually calmed down enough to walk in, deciding that I'm just acting weird, and that none of that really happened. She probably thinks I'm strange or crazy. Regardless, I think I'll avoid her for the rest of the night... Then forever after that. Yeah, that sounds like a good plan.

A few more hours ticked by as the last of my brother's fans left. Between weird guys hitting on me, and the stress of earlier events, I was so ready to get the hell out of there. I swear I felt her watching me non-stop the entire time. I'm Straight. I like guys. They're assholes, and I'm getting tired of them. But I'm not gay... I mean yeah, I look at women. I notice their beauty, and the size of their décolletage and the way their hips swing. Their soft voices and smooth skin. Their cunning eyes and how killer they look in red dresses. How sensual and sexual they can be at any given moment. That ache one feels when a woman stares at you from across the room, and you know that they like you far more than ever said. But that doesn't mean I'm instantly gay! That's not how that shit works. Women look at women, that's normal. So why the hell is her gaze turning me on? Why do my eyes search for her at every given chance? And why do I feel her immediately when she steps near me? Why does every guy in here handsome or not, pale next to her? As if she outshines them in every way. . . I am not gay!

My brother snapped me out of my daze. "Em, you ok? You've been acting strange today..." I turned towards him, ready to speak. He looked tired, his eyes a bit red. He spoke before I could. "Never mind, I'm sorry to ask you this but I have to pick Carrie up from the airport in..." He looked down at his watch. "Less than an hour and then I have to put Mike down for bed." Where is he going with this? "Could you stay and help clean?" Dammit!

"No, no and no" I stuck my chin out. He looked stressed. "Come on, please?" I stared at him. "I promise to make it up to you, but I could really use your help tonight sis." I sighed and gave him a smile. "Sure, what else am I good for, but you owe me." His relieved smile mocked my dreading frown on the inside. With that, he picked up my sleeping nephew and left. Left me. Alone. With. her. Alone. Please no.

So, he is handing me over on a platter, you know, I hate when my sarcasm is turned into reality. It really, really sucks. Slowly I turned around and faced her. She was casually leaning against a bookshelf with a type of glint in her dark eyes. "So, we meet again." I took a small step back. Why'd he ask me to stay? This place is nearly spotless. Yeah, there's some trash here and there. Stale food that needs thrown away... But, I don't wanna be here. "You know, I was wondering who his sweet little sister, Emma-Rose was. He talks often of you." Yeah, as his sacrificial offering, I'm sure. She reached up, and pulled a single, long silvery blue hairpin out of the top of her hair. Causing her wild ringlets to fall all around her. I was lost for words, as I felt myself being drawn into her again. The only thing I could focus on were her plush lips and the ever-growing wetness in my underwear. "I must say, in the many months I've known your brother, he failed to mention just how beautiful you were. And how curious." She smiled at me, her eyes ghosting down, then back up my body. Undressing me completely and causing me to shiver. "I should go..." I took another step back. Hoping the exit wasn't far. Pushing herself off the bookshelf, she approached me with quick long steps. Man, she has some really nice legs. That's not gay, women notice these types of things about other women. It's natural.

"I'd rather you didn't." She whispered, closer to me than I thought. When the hell did she get so close? Damn her sexy distracting legs! I was stuck in a trance; I should be running away. To where, I don't really know, but far away from her. I leaned back and looked up into her eyes, they had this look in them. As if she could see right into the fiber of my being, something inside my stomach shifted. "Why have you been avoiding me?" Is she talking? Gawd, why does her voice sound like sex? "I- I haven't..." I tried to lie in the face of perfection. She smirked down at me, resting her chin between her thumb and pointer. Her fingers were long, elegant. I wonder... "You are not a very good lair. You should work on that."

Her hand softly brushing my cheek snapped me into reality. "What?" I was disoriented, lost to her. The way she held herself made me feel weak, both mentally and physically. Like I needed her to be strong for me. Her warm fingers brushed over my eyes, forcing me to close them. My nose, then my lips, I sighed into her hand when it again rested on my cheek. "Very good" she whispered. I leaned into her hand, drifting towards her. when reality smacked me in the face. Whatever she's doing to me, I need to snap out of it. I am not gay!

I yanked away from her; my face warm with embarrassment. "I donno what you think I am, and hey I'm as gay positive as they come. But I'm not interested in whatever you're selling Mesa. So, I'm gonna go ahead and leave. Nice meeting you, or whatev' but I have to leave now." She looked surprised at the words that just left me, but I'm not sticking around to be hypnotized again. Proud at my superior ability at resisting a witch, I turned on my heels and began walking out. With visions of a tequila sunrise and a victory dance when her words stopped me.

"Sweet Emma, always the pride of all who meet her
The pride of vanity, like the veins that feed her
She walks on sunshine yet dances in the dark
For the wicked envies, the joy of her heart

Her smile which blinds like the light of day
Is haunted by her dreams where her shadows play
And oh sweet Emma, if tears do fall
Many would blindly jump, to catch them all

But she will float, like a feather to the ocean
Drifting by, as they drown on her potion."

I stood, dumbfounded by her poem. Then I snapped in rage. "That's bullshit! You don't know me!" I shouted, stomping up to her. I glared up at her, wanting to cause her pain. Her lips twitched up into a smirk. "Oh really?" she said, taking a step towards me. I jumped back. "You make me out to be some kind of monster! You know nothing about me." I stuck my chin out, ready for a fight.

She only smiled and took another step my way. "Oh Emma, I do not wish you harm. But the truth is what I speak." I glared at her. I know I'm somewhat spoiled and have never been at the bottom of the food chain. But that damn poem makes it sound like I'm two faced. "That's not true, I'm not that bad." I spoke, feeling the weight of her words... Her head leaned to the side.

"The truth does fall, from stranger's lips
Like a woman's kiss, or the sway of her hips
And all who listen, know this is true
Unlike those who are, just like you

Everything you think, is real and fake
Fades away like sand, upon a lake
They see and hear, but do not comprehend

For they destroy the things, they cannot mend

But listen not, to a witch's rhyme
We've only survived, through fire and time
We don't know anything, besides surviving
And tricking little girls,
Whose true self they are hiding."

"Shut up! I do listen, I don't know you and you sure as hell don't know me! Just stop! I... I..." Tears welled up in my eyes as her steady gaze held me down. "I'm not like that..." but even as I spoke, uncertainty tickled the edges to the point of discomfort. I quickly wiped away the tears. "Am I really that bad?" I mean, I can't say that I'm innocent... But, Argh!

Her voice stilled me as she spoke. "You are. However, you are but the product of your upbringing Emma. They have treated you like the rot of a queen your entire life. You know no other way. But, if you'll allow me, I can show you a path unlike one you have ever imagined." I looked down, unsure of what to say or do. Wondering if her words, though hurtful, were honest. Am I rotten? I thought of my ex-boyfriend, I currently have no sympathy over that disaster. My brother and nephew love me. I am loved, but as my mind wandered, and past lovers and lost friends drifted forward. How I directed and controlled. Then managed to walk away when I wasn't pleased with the outcomes. Selfish, spoiled, self-centered, heartless... All things people have called me and more that I quickly discounted over the years.

My chest ached, I never analyzed myself before. And this isn't exactly the first time I've been called out, but for some reason, her words weighed the heaviest. They forced me to confront myself. I slowly backed away, her words wrapping around me like tendrils of smoke. Locking my hands to my side. Again, the feeling of suffocation enveloped me, and I can't even run! I stood, bound by the weight of her words alone. I should have run out when I had the chance to. Because now she stood in front of me, her eyes blazing in swirls of dark blue, like murky waters without a seeable end. She stood; a small smile turned up the corner of her red lips. "You will not resist me this time, little one." Was all she said, causing my knees to weaken. All of my defenses fell from my lips in an unintelligible mumble. As I felt myself being pulled towards her.

In that moment, I forgot why I wanted to run. Why I was so hell bent on getting away from her. She makes my skin tingle all over my body, and it's fascinating. She makes me feel... different. Standing straight she turned around. "Follow me, I would like to show you something." Nodding dumbly, I followed her. The tendrils pulling me after, not letting me go. Guiding my way and soothing all my fears. Thinking of nothing but the growing hunger in my gut. This pressing attraction that I've never felt so strongly. I believe she is leading me to my doom, but try as I might, I just can't stop my legs from following her. I almost didn't want to stop. Her hips swayed with an air of power. They swished and rotated in a hypnotic way, making it extremely difficult to focus on anything but her.

I think I want her. It sounds completely crazy and foreign, but nonetheless, possibly true. This beautiful witch is tempting me straight to the darkness I once feared. And she's right, I can't resist her. A haze filled my vision, and my heart hummed. She led me to the same wooden door. The door that has opened up unseen possibilities. Only she didn't stop there. She continued towards another door to the side. She led me into a darkened room, lit only by candlelight. I looked around confused. I hadn't notice this here before, but then again how do you notice anything with a woman like her humping her own fingers?

There were no windows in here. It smelled sweet, and earthy, both inviting and intoxicating. On the walls hung sensual pictures of women in silhouette, styling erotic poses. The sight of this room surprised me. Though I'm not sure what I would have expected... Maybe more books, not a giant bed with beautiful blue sheets. Coming up behind me, she brushed her fingers down my arms, resting her hands on them. My skin ignited to life, tingling everywhere she touched. I felt like I was again in her trance as she turned me around and gently pushed me back until the wall stopped me. Nervously, I fought the spell she had put me under, and managed to utter out a small "What are you doing?"

She smiled at me, like the queen she is, and whispered against my ear. "I am going to give to you what you have denied of yourself, your entire life little girl. And then, I am going to expand your concept of fact and fiction." I've never truly acknowledged my attraction to women. N-never was daring enough to want to try. But the way her eyes looked down at me, made my heart palpitate. Made the darkness I've kept hidden, rise to the surface. "Let me explain my desire to you, Sweet Emma" she said in a seductively husky voice, making my clit twitch in response. "You have a power within you. One that attracts me to you. Your intelligence, your beauty, the scent that flows off your skin and perfumes around the room..." She paused, "This alone makes a part of me grow restless. And it takes all of my restraint not to ravish you where you stand. I want to hold you down and take all that I want from you... I want you burning for me, begging...I want to unlock that power you've kept hidden within you. And watch it burn all the lies from your knowledge." She smiled with a moderate dose of sauciness.

"Ahem... Back to the pressing matter at hand." She said as she squeezed her hands tighter on my waist. "I am a woman of pride, and I would like to claim you." She leaned in closer. Her chest pressing against mine. "To hold you tight while you moan out my name. I desire to cause you to make wetness, for you to unravel beneath me... perhaps, for you to be mine..." She was looking into my eyes with a fire. "And I have not wanted to make a woman do that in quite some time... I understand that I am being forward, but I want to hear you confess your hidden truths, Emma. I want you to hang onto me, in clutches of ecstasy while I ravish you. I want you to be so completely overwhelmed with the pleasure I cause you, that you lose control. That who you think you are, erupts and empties out all over my bed, and all over me." Her eyes held every intention of honesty as she spoke. Not looking away, not even once as she shattered my perception of what a woman could do.

What the actual, natural fuck? My clit, now on full alert, my breath getting stuck behind a lump in my throat. I... I can't believe this... N-no woman should want to do those things to me. I shouldn't want her to do those things. Yet... yet the thought of her holding me down undeniably turned me on more than I thought possible. I wanted it, the forbidden temptation that she was. I wanted to taste her truths, even if they dragged me down. I had a hundred questions. Such as, what power was she talking about? How come she hasn't wanted other women? Why is she attracted to me? Why am I attracted to her? Why is she so strong? How insane is she? Did she escape from a mental hospital? And can I taste her lips?...

But none of these questions came to my mouth as she continued her unwavering gaze. Stripping me down to the bone and analyzing the troubled remains. She leaned back and looked down at me. Her eyes looking somewhere deep within my being. The corner of her mouth was turned up into a seductive smirk, she released me, causing cold air to rush and chill the space her warmth once was. She then placed her hands on the wall behind me. Goosebumps scattered across my cooling skin. "Will you allow me the privilege to give you pleasure Emma-Rose?" My hands shook as if I were standing at the edge of a cliff, and she was telling me to jump. "Will you release your power and let me take you?" Heart racing, palms sweating... I felt my head nodding, the sweet fumes of the candles making me lightheaded. Unable to do more than that simple movement, my tongue stuck to the roof of my mouth. She leaned in closer, her lips brushing against mine. My heart going crazy inside of my chest. "Say it" She whispered, her breath fanned over my face, smelling of mint and wine. "Y-yes"

My voice was shaking, my clit throbbing, but I managed to say it. A light shined in her dark blue eyes, like an underwater pool light. Her lips brushed mine again, sending small shock waves throughout my nervous system. "So be it, my little witch." She said with a sparkle in her eyes.

She stepped back and turned away from me "Unzip me, will you?" Ahh! Freaking out! I'm definitely freaking out! She stood with her back to me. Her strong shoulders defined in the soft, flickering light of the room. She glanced over her shoulder at me, her eyes drawing me forward without a single word spoken. I found myself moving, shaking hands and all as I grasped her zipper and pulled it down. It ran down her spine to the very bottom of her lower back. Showing off her beautiful, olive skin. The sexy dip of her hips, and the sensual curve of her strong back. I was again lost for words. She had the shoulders of a swimmer, the back of a professional gymnast, and the grace of a ballerina. Her muscles flexed with each movement, something that would instantly cause every man to envy, and every woman to swoon. My mouth watered as light flickered off her toned muscles and danced upon her tattoos. Revealing tribal markings and designs I couldn't interpret. A dragon climbed up her back, releasing its fire along the left side of her stomach.

She took a step forward, then turned to face me. Letting her dress drop to the ground. Under it she was as nude as the day of her blessed birth. Her breasts, without anything added, were beyond perfect. They weren't huge, they simply claimed their ground. Standing proudly without needing assistance from a bra, clearly defying gravity. Her soft looking areolas watched me, her nipples demanding attention. The softness of her tattooed stomach, the black curly hair of her mons. She was the vision of a goddess, a fallen angel, a rising devil. And the wicked smile that curved her lips up, led me to believe that I was not wrong. I watched her with wide eyes as she winked at me, then turned around and approached a desk adorned with a black cloth, a few unlit candles, a silver bowl, and a pitcher of water. Her body was beautifully molded, and those interesting tribal tattoos climbed up her leg, and sides.

She didn't say a word, and I couldn't seem to move, couldn't even think of the command that would have allowed it. I stayed there, planted in the same spot she left me. I-I think I might be drooling, she was, no, is a beautiful creature. Her skin flawless, her eyes entrapping, her lips enticing, her curves, her muscles... I just don't understand it. Why am I feeling both lust and fear for her? It's like she's the big bad wolf... and I am nothing more than her play toy, her prey. She lit the remaining candles and filled the bowl with water as if a ritual. Placing her fingertips into the water and chanting lightly under her breath. My mind immediately played a trick on me, making me think that the water started to glow a soft blue. Clearly, I'm hallucinating, and obviously need mental help. Once done she made her way back to me. "You truly are a wonder Emma. Oh so gifted." She placed her hand on my shoulder and gently pushed me until I could move back no further. "Are you sure you want this Emma? You will not be the same when I am done with you." Gulping nervously, I nodded, accepting my fate. Though I wasn't sure at all. She smiled in approval, tilting her head to the side.

"I must inform you, Emma. If you speak of anything that happens here, outside of my ears, you will not appreciate the outcome. I have skills and abilities that I'd rather not have shared with the world. Because if you do talk, I will come after you. I will make you suffer. I will show no mercy, and your existence will be no more." Okay, did I mention fear? That's its cold touch, pricking the back of my neck. What the hell is she talking about?!?! I nodded quickly at her; she looks like the type to actually go through with her threats. And I could almost feel the air chilling around her.

"That is good. Now, one last thing, sweet Emma. If I find out from this point on, that you've willingly involved yourself with a male, I will touch you no longer. Our fun will end. I am not a jealous lover, but I will not share you with the opposite sex. If you wish to test me, I would advise against it. Emma, you can end this at any point. But listen carefully, when you end it, it will not happen again. Do you understand?" Am I the only one not completely understanding this? I wanted to say no, that I don't understand. But as she spoke her hand gently moved up and down my sides. Did I mention that she's naked? Oh sweet goddess, I can't even focus on her words!

"I will not make another move without your agreement..." Her fingertips continued their slow hypnosis, gently drifting with the lightness of a feather over my skin. She caused a tickle deep inside me. A fire that burned brighter than anyone has been able to cause before. And I realized that I don't always have to know or understand. But in this moment, what I wanted was more than I've ever had. And she possibly could give it to me. "U-understood" I whispered. This seemed to make her happy, I wanted to observe her, she's interesting, the way she carries herself. She leaned in closer to me and kissed my cheek, her lips softly causing a warmth to spread beneath my skin "I could be very rough, I could be mean... but I will be gentle. I will show you the true joys and secrets of the sexual arts." She brushed her lips up closer to my ear and whispered "I will corrupt you, then I will entice you to the wonderment of my world. Last, I will teach you of the power only dreamt of in your storybooks." My entire body vibrated with excitement; I could use some corruption. She began kissing down my neck, sliding her warm tongue along my skin. The feeling of that alone made me breathless as I squeezed my legs together, trying to control the hormones rushing through me. Turns out, that's utterly pointless.

Her hand drifted up, brushing over my nipple, and as if by her magic touch alone, it hardened with nothing more than a ghosting pass. A direct line from the tip of my now rock-hard points, went straight down to my continuously throbbing clit. Which has been begging for attention for a while now. My fingers itched to touch myself, but she had me pinned, her warm body pressed tightly against mine. She lightly grazed her fingertips over my hardened nipple again, pinching it lightly between her fingers, then a little harder. I tried to stifle a moan as her tongue slid across my bottom lip. "Do not fight the pleasure you feel. Let it guide you, let it set you free." She spoke against my lips. I moaned again, her voice, that voice. It's the voice of Sex! She pressed her body hard against mine, pulling my head back by my hair. I winced. Her teeth not so softly scraped along my exposed neck.

"El-yie Ahhb-suh Cah-neh Room-muh Coo Chay-ahv El-yie Nah-shuh-see, El-yie Ahhb-suh Oo-oh-tah Coo Dee-eh Mull Me-tah Coo Tell-kah Ah-two-oh Ee-shah-may"

I squeezed my eyes closed, trying to make sense of the nonsense she was speaking. The beautifully formed words held no meaning as they drifted in a sing-song like whisper, causing my body to rise in heat. She repeated the last part. Her body rocking hard into mine with each word. "Ee-nah?" she asked, her head leaning back, her eyes storming with some type of deep emotions. I know she asked a question, but I'm completely confused as to what she asked. Again, she said the same thing. "Ee-nah?" her eyes watching me closely. I couldn't speak as her other hand found its way up my skirt, almost two months of me touching myself, this felt too good to speak. Her long fingers pushed my panties aside and opened my lips. The cool air now chilled my exposed opening as her fingers teased my clit. She bent down, lifted up my shirt, and nibbled on my nipple through my bra. The assault of pleasure blocked out the fact that I was in a dark room, against a wall, in a bookstore, with a powerful, dominate woman. Key word being, WOMAN.

"I don't know what to say." A mischievous smile spread across her red lips. "You say, 'nahh'" I stared up at her, she seemed to be waiting for my reply. I'd agree to just about anything if she asked. But first, "What language is... what are you speaking in?"

She rested her forehead on mine, her eyes not moving from me. "It is the language of my people. As timeless as time itself. It is the language of beauty, sex, lust, and strength. The language of warriors... My people..." She said the last few words with sadness, it swirled in her eyes. Shined there like unspilled tears. I was overwhelmed by her, her strength, her presence, and the fact that she doesn't hide her emotions. It's clear that this upsets her, and she lets it show. Her people, can't she just go home? I suppose, maybe it's not that simple.

She stood straight, her eyes asking a silent question. I took a deep breath, nodded and repeated "nahh?" a smile bloomed across her face. "Nahh" she replied. Then she tilted my chin up, speaking softly. "I will take from you as I desire, I will fill you with my liquid. You are now mine." I immediately wanted to question what she meant by that, but my wonderings were immediately silenced by her lips. My clit instantly hardened to the point of pain and quickly became sensitive to her touch. Her fingers grasped my clit, causing a gasp of shock to jump out of me. She moved back down to my nipple and continued nibbling, making my eyes roll up into my head. She kept a tight hold of my clit. Barely pushing and pulling her hand slowly. Effectively giving me my first hand-job. I didn't even know that was possible! Grinding onto her hand I closed my eyes, letting the pleasure overtake me.

It pulsed and coursed through my veins, I arched back, pushing my breasts towards her. But she released it, the cold almost hurting as it surrounded my now swollen flesh. I looked into her eyes as she released my clit, causing a strangled cry to leave me. "Oh, is there a problem sweet Emma? Have I stopped too soon?" I bit my lip. Not sure how to respond. She chuckled and entered one long finger smoothly into me. I instantly clenched around her, drowning in the feeling of bliss. "Mmm, little one, you have been wanting this. Your body calls to me." I shuddered at the lust in her voice. Her single digit seemed to fill me more than any of my exes ever could. She then began her agonizingly slow assault inside of me. Pushing her finger all the way in. Then slowly pulling it all the way out. She's trying to drive me mad! And succeeding quite successfully. Pulling me to the edge of sanity. I whimpered, thrusting my hips forward, trying to gain more from the little she gave. My breathing was erratic and heart beating too fast. She slammed her lips onto mine. Effortlessly slipping her tongue in as she sped her movements. Her tongue explored my mouth, taking full advantage over me. The way it turned and moved vaguely reminded me of a snake, I guess the oddest part being that I enjoyed it so much. Her skill alone could shame a player and kill a Saint.

I felt the burning of need in my gut. The curl of my fingers and toes, the building pressure in my core that told me I'm close! She then curved her finger up, abusing my G spot with little mercy. I rocked harder onto her as her thumb brutally teased my clit in the best possible way. I cried out as the orgasm rocked through me. Slamming back against the wall, eyes closed, my chest burned, my legs shook, my head spun. I clenched around her finger with each pulse of my release. My own clit caused me to jump, every time it twitched. A deep wanting throb followed, drawing out a moan. She removed her lips from mine, sliding her expert tongue from my mouth. Then her wonderful finger. I think if I knew it'd be this good with a woman, I would never have been with a guy. Why are we not promoting and advertising this!

"You released quickly; it must have been a while... However, I seek to change that... To build your endurance. But that will not be today, today, I want to hear you scream." She brought her fingers up, wet with my juices and licked them clean. Her tongue, longer than I have ever seen, sensually wrapped around her finger. I'm not breathing... I should be breathing but I'm not. She smiled at me then managed to remove the rest of my clothing without me being able to say a single word. I didn't have the strength to stop her... or even want to. Why would I? Yes, she's a woman, but this woman got me off quicker than I thought possible. And without me having to allow my mind to wonder. Once done, I too stood naked in front of her. My clothing now a pool of fabric at my feet. She grabbed ahold of my right thigh, lifting it up, and resting it on her hip. Causing me to stand on my toes. "What are you...?" I started to speak, but I was silenced as she pushed something warm, smooth, and hard right into me. I screamed as it burrowed its way further in. I felt it stretching me wide, filling me up and twitching inside of me. Pressing into every pressure point within my lower body. I winced in pain, trying not to move. A moan as soulful as jazz and as sexy as chocolate left her red lips. Her eyes were dilated, her cheeks pink as she pushed it further into me. I whimpered, trying to relax to accommodate the size of her toy. I thought Lesbians only used fingers. Hahaha, WRONG!

Once it was all the way in, she stopped moving. I couldn't help how my muscles clenched around it, trying to squeeze it out. The odd thing is... When I clenched, she moaned. I did it again and she moaned out, hissing as she rested her head on my shoulder. "Relax, take a deep breath, then let it out slowly." She whispered roughly, trying to catch her breath. I did as she said, again and again till the pain seemed to ease. "Good girl" I won't lie, I'm completely confused... But hey, I haven't really taken a good look at the dildo selections. I bet they can do a shit ton of odd things now.

She lifted her head up and stared into my eyes. Her eyes swirled with emotion as she slowly moved the dildo slowly back and forth in me. My body vibrated with pain mixed with pleasure. Layered with a heavy dose of need, as her moves gently picked up speed. The way she was moaning with every thrust had me questioning reality. Could this much pleasure truly be happening, and how can I possibly be processing this without blacking out. But I was soon overtaken with pleasure, I quickly forgot about it and matched her thrust for thrust, as I became lost in her eyes. She smirked at me, and before I could form a questioning thought, she hoisted me onto her. I instinctively wrapped my legs around her waist to keep me up. Damn, she's strong, her muscles flexed as she held me tight, causing me to swoon over her. I love strength, always have found it to be amazingly attractive. And she has it in both mind and body.

Pushing me back against the wall she grabbed my hips and slammed hard into me. Black dots filled my vision, as I struggled to breathe. Throwing my head back I began moaning out, tears slipping from my eyes. It's never felt this good; I've never had more than one orgasm when not by myself. Already I was rapidly approaching my next. The sound of her heavy breathing and my ass repeatedly hitting the wall filled the room and echoed off the walls.

"Say my name, give yourself to me. Be mine." She huskily spoke as she pumped inhumanly faster into me. "M-Mesa!" I moaned out, trying to focus and not being able to. My lower half burned and throbbed in pleasure, my head spinning. "Please don't stop" I begged. It felt odd and a little dirty, but in this moment, I'd call her the freaking Pope if she wanted me to. I clawed at her back, her skin on mine felt so good, amazing even. "Surrender yourself to me Emma." I squeezed my eyes closed, feeling the overwhelming effects of her all over me. The words fell from my lips, and seemingly from my chest. "I am yours; you possess me." A growling like sound left her, rumbling into my soul. Inflaming me, engulfing me whole.

"Your body belongs to me now Emma. You are mine, and I am yours." Her words only brought me closer, shredding away my concept of reality. "Who do you belong to?" She asked just before biting into my neck whilst rotating her hips. "You!" I cried, so much pleasure it felt like pain, pumped into my blood stream. "Whose body is this?" She stopped moving entirely. "Yours" I whispered. "You. Are. Mine. Understood?" I am hers. The toy seemed to grow inside of me, pulling and stretching to fill my space. I gasped in shock, holding on tight to her shoulders "Nahhh!" I cried out, holding my breath. Smiling triumphantly, she slammed back into me with a death grip on my hips, no doubt leaving bruises. But it only pushed me closer. "You will release your liquid to me." She moaned in my ear. She was sweating, her black curls clung damply to her skin as her eyes watched my face for any sign. Pulling her closer I moaned deeply, she shuddered against me, pushing harder into me. Anymore and I might split in half. "I-I" I moaned, "I'm cumming!" I bit my lip hard as heat burst from within me. The slick sounds of her pushing in and out of me, rang in my ears. She continued to thrust in, intensifying my already strong orgasm. She latched onto my shoulder, biting hard as she moaned out. My whole body shook, mind blank of everything except her. I moaned louder, my body twitching with the intense release that rocked me. My core throbbed and pulsed then an interesting feeling washed through me as shots of liquid hotness filled me down below. She was moaning, her eyes closed, her toy jumping inside of me. At first, I simply enjoyed it. The way she filled me, the way I slumped against her. Too tired to think or move. Her hands alone kept me up. I was exhausted, and weak. My mind quickly fading into the warm afterglow I love.

"You will stay in my bed tonight Me-mah-he." She said as she slowly pulled out of me. Then, like a ton of bricks hitting me, the realization of what just happened slapped me unexpectedly. She just came inside of me with a toy. And she felt it. She, she came... What. The. Fuck.

A fearful whimper left me, as I began shaking. Too afraid to look down, too terrified at what I might find... Hopefully, it's all in my imagination. B-because I saw her masturbating. So of course, it's all in my imagination. She has everything I have. So, it's just a really good toy. Maybe one of those double-sided dildos I've heard of. Yeah, that makes sense.

Feeling better about my silly freak out, I whispered her word for yes. She smiled triumphantly, her eyes twinkling "Kind dreams sweet Emma. I will protect you as you sleep." I smiled and laid my head on her shoulder. Feeling the warmth of exhaustion dragging down my eyelids as she effortlessly carried me away. And for the first time in my adult life, as she laid me down on soft sheets, pressed against her warm body, I fell asleep before my lover. And drifted into a world unknown. Inside of a hidden room, at the back of the Impulse Bookstore. Next to a woman. Damn.

☒

## Chapter 3

# Snippet: Beg

I stared down at my pet. Her legs spread open for me. Her chest rising and falling as she tried to cope with the emotions I was invoking within her. She's so beautiful, so innocent. Had she known what I was capable of, I am certain she would have never come my way. I should let her go... But I won't.

I am going to do things to her, I am going to make her scream my name. Beg for release. And once I've gotten her at the very edge, right at the brink of her an orgasm, I'm going to stop. I am going to tease her while she rides the edge, while she begs desperately for mercy. And then and only then will I give her release, and it will shatter through her, crumbling her restraint. Her sweet body rocked unceremoniously against the vibration between her smooth thighs. The scent of her arousal filling the room. Her hands tied above her head, her eyes blindfolded. Her body still rocking. Mmm, that's it my sweet pet, moan in unquenched need.

I sat in my chair, enjoying the view. The vibrator just barely close enough to buzz her lips. She's wet, I can see the shine of her natural lubricant from here. Slowly, with my legs spread over the armrests of my chair, I enticed my clit. Her whimpers of frustration making my own core pulse in joy. I could relieve her, could make it easy and quick. But what fun would that be? Watching her suffer for her own pleasure is much too liberating. Mmm... A moan broke from me, as I rocked gently on my fingertips. I can hear the leather creek as she pulls against her restraints. She knows what I want to hear, so proud, this one. All the better for me.

My clit was hard beneath my fingers. Not as hard as hers is right now. I'm close, so close. But I stop just before releasing. I would be a terrible hostess if I relieved myself before relieving her. Bringing my fingers to my lips, I tasted myself. Savoring the sinful taste of my own essence. Standing up, I walked toward the bed. My boots clicking on the hardwood floor. She slowed her actions down. So very unaware of what I am going to do for her. Her lips trembled, her body shimmering with a thin sheen of sweat. "Please" she begged softly, her muscles tense, she's on edge. She is beautiful, her curved hips, the sensual swell of her breasts that jiggled a bit with each rapid inhale.

She wants something she has never had. Something she has yet to grasp. Something only I can give... I observed her as she yet again pulled on her restraints. Not truly aware of how close I am to her. Bending down, I placed my lips against hers. Catching her off guard, she gasped, but didn't jump back. "That's a good girl" I whispered against her warm lips. My own curved up into a smile. I slowly glided my hand down her abdomen, a soft whimper leaving her pink lips. "Please Mistress, please." Her begging was hitting me in all the right spots.

"Such a naughty girl, getting so turned on by being tied up. I bet no one would ever guess that a good girl like you would be this pervy. What would they say if they knew? Huh bad girl? You get off on this, don't you?" At first, she didn't reply. Her head shaking back and forth as I neared her slit. Her whimpers increasing as her hips picked up speed. She was like fire down at her lower lips. Her sweet nectar practically dripping from her need. I slid my fingers down her slit and into her inner lips. Her hips jerked up to meet me as I brushed her pulsing pearl. "Mmm, for one who denies her own pleasure, you sure seem to want this. To crave what I can do for you." She was biting her bottom lip hard. I growled and grabbed her clit tightly between my fingers, making her cry out.

"Say it" I demanded. Her whole body shook with need as her words fell from her lips. "I need this Mistress! Please, please give me relief!" I smile victoriously. "I don't think the neighbors heard you just yet naughty girl. Try a little louder."

She whimpered, pulling harder, hips wiggling with more urgency. "Please mistress! I need you. I can't take much more!" Her lips trembled. I lightened my grip on her clit, gently running my nail along the hardened nub. Mmm... "Such a good Submissive."

Chapter 4

# No Privacy

Finally! I have a moment to myself... I haven't gone nearly this long without at least a little bit of self-medication. Also known as masturbation. And it's been over a month! I peeked over the edge of my bunk at my cell mate. Her soft breathing was deep, her eyes closed, her chest slowly moving. I gotta say, I'm lucky. She keeps me protected and doesn't try to force herself on me. I honestly think she's just waiting for me to wear down, which isn't surprising. She's a beautiful chocolate woman, tall and strong. Her thick hair braided back artistically. I sighed in relief, happy that she's asleep. With a smile, I rolled onto my back. It's hard writing the stories I write, seeing the things I see. Feeling the need I have... And not doing anything about it! They keep me tense and, on the edge, constantly. Pushing me up against walls and whispering highly suggestive things in my ears. They grab me at times and kiss me as if I'm the most fucking desirable thing in this whole damn prison, then just walk away like nothing happened. I'm just so frustrated! I need to at least rub! But no, I'm usually watched like a snitch, constantly observed as they read in indulgence of the stories they force me to write! It's how I pay for protection in this place. Little stories of lust, sex, and naughtiness to keep from getting beaten, raped, or killed. Honestly, I think I might have it easy. But they're all in cahoots! Keeping me in a crazed state of arousal. But now is my time!

Quickly, I slipped my hand under the waistband of my orange pants and eased a finger between my folds. Instantly my body jolted alive at the sweet sensation of my fingertip brushing my clit. I couldn't help the small moan, or how quickly my eyes closed in bliss. This is how I know I've gone too long. I went from rubbing almost every day to this... Grasping at the tiniest of moments of bliss in passing seconds... I've fallen quite low for being the sex fiend that I am... At least my orgasm will be amazing.

I was already wet, moist from a hard clit being ignored for an extended period of time. I was hot, the throbbing between was begging me to continue. I lightly grazed my clit again, torturing myself a little further. Making me want it more. I couldn't possibly want it any more than I do now. But I've always enjoyed the tease, cherished the chase. My legs widened, my heart picking up pace. I positioned my fingers just right and started moving them gently in small circles. My hips reacted all on their own. Moving back and forth against my slick fingers. Making my pulsing clit harder. I tried to stay as quiet as possible. This is the ultimate pleasuring high of a solo performance. The thrill of being naughty, the fear of getting caught, the underlying current of wanting to, and the blinding joy of reaching peak O!

I licked my dry lips, the pleasure spreading rapidly throughout my body. I feel warm, too much clothing. But I didn't stop, I rubbed harder even as my walls clenched for more. Unable to help myself, I teased my opening. Tracing the outline with my finger. My other hand moved up my body, my nails gently scraping along my skin. Awakening my flesh, exciting me as my hand came to rest on my chest. I traced up my mound, grazing my palm over my erect nipple then giving it a not so gentle pinch. I gasped, overtaken by the pleasure and plunged my waiting fingers into me. A shaky whimper escaped my lips as I struggled to control my breathing. My hips rose off the bed in a desperate attempt to take more than what I could give myself.

Holy heavens, this feels so good. I've missed this. For a moment, I forgot where I was. Who I was, and just gave into the pleasure. Women's faces and bodies flashed in my mind. Women holding me down. Telling me to take it. And me, me taking it. Me taking it and loving the pain mixed with an even greater pleasure. I was so close, everything seemed to stop, except me finishing. My mind and body screamed for release as another moan left me, this time it was unashamed. I opened my eyes into the darkened room of my cell, looking up at the concrete ceiling, rocking harder. Closer to my goal. Closer to my release. So close. My head fell to the side, ready to go the next step. Ready to grasp something so beautiful only the bold could touch. I momentarily opened my eyes again, and they locked with hers. My heart jumped, and blood chilled within me. She stood across the room, leaning against the wall, watching me. Her arms folded; a smirk carved onto her lips. I froze, in disbelief, in fear, in... in... in shock. How long has she been watching me?

A whimper fell from my lips. Do I stop?! I... I can't stop! It's been so long! I've been moody, on edge, and I need this! No, I can't stop now, I'm not stopping! I was breathing heavy, my heart raced. I watched her, locked in the tango of wills. She thinks I'll stop, as I have so many times before. Not this time. Biting my bottom lip, I pushed my fingers back into me. Her smirk faded away as she watched me intensely. I moaned, forcing my eyes to stay open, and pushing harder. My eyes looked over her. She's so strong, so capable. She could hold me down easily, without question.

She'd make me take what she could give, and I'd be almost helpless to stop her. I moaned out, the thought causing warm liquid to seep out of me. I closed my eyes now, ignoring the audience, as I neared my release. Her glare burning into my vision. Breathing harder, I pinched my nipple and attacked my clit. A hot ball of heat snaked down my body. Burning my insides. Close, so close! Struggling to focus, overwhelmed by the pleasure I've craved for so long as it shook my body. My hips jerked up, as hotness seemed to pour out of me. My clit jumped and pulsed with each passing second. My heart slamming against my chest. My breathing slowed as I lowered myself down. My head spinning, my skin chilling from the thin layer of sweat. The bed beneath me was damp.

I jumped when a hand slid across my midsection. Alarmed, I looked over and she was standing next to my bunk, on the ladder, watching me. Her hand gliding across my now exposed stomach. She grabbed a hold of my wrist and pulled my hand from beneath my waistband. I watched, frozen, unsure of what she was going to do. Pulling my hand close to her, she sniffed my wet fingers, inhaling my scent. Her tongue then poked out and teased the tip of my middle finger. Just flicking the end. Causing my soft clit to throb back to life. Without saying a word, she gently pushed my hand towards me. Placing the tip of my fingers to my mouth. I looked at her, uncertain. "Suck" she said, and nothing more. Overwhelmed with the warmth of my orgasm and the power of her demand, I opened my mouth, as she pushed my fingers inside of me. I moaned at the familiar earthy taste of my own essence. Licking my juices off my fingers. Her eyes didn't leave me. She watched intensely, growling a bit even. She then pulled my fingers from my mouth, and slipped one of hers in. A part of me wanted to flinch away. But her intense gaze held me there as I gently sucked the tip of her finger. "You and I, Beautiful, are going to get along just fine." She said. Pushing her finger deeper into my mouth. "Now suck harder, you sexy little wordsmith. I want to feel more of that lovely tongue of yours."

⊠

## Chapter 5

# Caught

I sat in the living room with my brother's friend Chelsie. Why am I with my brother's friend Chelsie? Well, the idiot invited her over to play games or whatever but forgot about it and went to the mall before she even got here. Now I'm stuck with her because her Mom drove off like a bat out of hell before we could flag her down. And to add onto it, De took my car so I can't drive her home. Just my luck, I really wanted to enjoy myself today. I sighed sadly. I only ever get to do it when everyone's gone or asleep. This was my chance! I really need to move out, sooner rather than later. A bit more upset than I should have been, I unlocked my phone and went to the search bar. Might as well occupy myself with a little entertainment. "Lesbians" I looked at the images and smiled.

The couch shifted, I looked over at her. She's about two years younger than I am. She's beautiful, there's just something about her. A hidden something that I can't figure out... She had that perfect 'girl next door' look, with dark, thick ringlets and beautiful milk chocolate eyes. Her eyes were only intensified by her beautiful golden skin. I'm sure in eight or so years, when she comes back from college, De will see her and fall in love. And she'll fall for him too. You know, typical girl and boy love story... I continued to look at her, with my head tilted to the side. I was finding the thought of De loving her more and more disturbing. I shook my head, no way. I refuse to like my kid brother's friend. I bit my lip and looked down at my phone.

Doesn't matter. I'll be out of the house next year anyways. Then they can do whatever they want. I sat playing on my phone... well, not really playing. I was now looking at some pretty intense lesbian porn. My mom would freak if she knew, no one knows. And I'd like it to stay that way, at least until I leave, then I won't care. "Can I watch some TV?" She asked as I scrolled through the pictures.

"Sure, the remote is on the table, help yourself." I said without looking up. The couch cushions moved as she reached for it. I looked at her from under my eyelashes. She was wearing soft blue jeans and a light blue t-shirt. Her curly hair was pulled back into a ponytail. I sighed on the inside. She always had this effect on me, to cause me to focus on her when all I wanted is to have nothing to do with her. Her sweetness, her smile, the way she jokes and laughs...

Reluctantly, my eyes returned to my phone, the ladies beauty seemed to pale next to Chelsie's. But I was drawn to it, their sexuality, and the raw power they possessed. I licked my lips as I became engrossed with them. Running my thumb over the screen, I scanned countless images of them. My breathing increased as my hormones grew. I felt the all too familiar ache in my core. The slow throb that begged me to give into it. And give it what it needs. I clenched, causing my body to shake in need.

I glanced at Chelsie. Her eyes were glued to the TV. I slowly moved my hand in between my legs. As everything in me screamed to do it! But I stopped myself. Dammit! I can't do this with her right here! "Umm, Kelly?" I jumped, standing up looking down at her. "Hey, I'll be back." I held my phone to my ear, "I gotta take this call" she stared at me with disbelief in her eyes. ".... okay..."

I looked at her a bit confused but tossed it to the wind. I need to relieve myself, and at this point any lame excuse will do. I walked away as fast as I could to my room. With the door closed, I basked in my freedom. And slowly stripped to a comfortable nakedness. Then jumped into my bed. I love the way my sheets feel against my naked skin, I can't wait to leave this place, go to college, be free. I skimmed through a few more photos, gently touching myself. Before turning on my favorite porn video. Already wet, and excited, I slid my hand down my body, spreading my folds open. Heat radiated from my kitten, I repressed a moan, in fear that she would hear me. I watched the video of the two women in bed, one eating out the other. I lightly rubbed my pearl. Sending a zing of excitement throughout my entire body.

My clit was hard, warm, smooth and slick. My fingers were quickly coated in my own juices. I bit my lip and arched my back as I rubbed a little harder. My mind raced; I closed my eyes. My hips bucked up and my legs spread open. I allowed the thought of a naked Chelsie on top of me. I moaned deeply, massaging my breast with my free hand. The thought of her kissing my neck, running her hands hungrily across my nakedness.

My whole body was hot for her, as it rocked against my hand. In my mind, she spread open her legs, and began grinding on top of me. Her hot wetness running down my stomach as she road me like a cowgirl. My clit jumped as I ran my nails over the tips of my nipples. My breathing was ragged. My body shook as I neared my release. My own hot wetness seeped out of me the closer I got. A deep burning filled my core. My movements turning erratic and jerky. I pressed hard against my pulsing clit. Pushing with all I had in me, it took everything in me not to call her name in ecstasy.

Sweet release shook my body as I laid spent. Trying to calm my rapid breathing, I took deep slow breaths. My lower core pulsed as my clit grew sensitive, my nipples tender. A slow, easy smile spread across my lips, I reached into my bedside table and pulled out a victory joint. No time like the present time to get a little high. I only took a few puffs of it, holding it in, then released it in a long stream of thick, white smoke. With a lazy smile, I put it out and slid it back into its little lock box. In moments like this, alone and happy, it does feel like life is good. Getting up, I got dressed and went into the bathroom to wash my hands. I straightened my hair and clothes. Smiling at the glow my skin had after my orgasm. I grabbed my phone and made my way back to the living room. Completely happy in my ability to rub and cum without being caught, I sat snuggly on the couch getting ready to open my phone.

"Umm...Kelly?" I looked up at Chelsie with a smile. "Yes?" Without saying a word, she pointed to the TV. I followed her finger and distinctly felt all the blood drain from my face. I looked down at my phone and unlocked it. Sure enough, the TV mirrored my screen. I never turned off my casting from last night.

Oh fuck. "Sooo, you had a call you say?" I looked back at Chelsie. Her whole demeanor seemed to change. Instead, there sat a confident woman in her place. Her pink lips turned up into that of a Cheshire cat like smile. "I... I... Uhh..." she smirked, her eyes sparkling. "What's wrong Kells? Kitty got your tongue?" I was stuck, lost for all words and excuses. She stood up, rising off the couch with a look I couldn't read lurking in her eyes. What is she going to do? Expose me? Blackmail me? "Looks like I have a bad girl on my hands. I didn't realize that you batted for my team Kelly, but I can't say I'm surprised..." She paused with a thoughtful expression as she stood in front of me, caging me in. "You and I are cut from the same cloth, might as well intertwine." She's a Lesbian?! Holy shit! Her lips crashed into mine, temporarily silencing my thoughts. Exploding my world with fascination and fear. I couldn't help but savor the taste and savor the moment. That is, until reality hit. I, Kelly Abrams, am currently making out with my brother's best friend!

And again, I say FUCK!

☒

## Chapter 6

# Snippet: Mistress

I laid in bed and closed my eyes. I could see her, my made-up Mistress. And in my mind's eye, she walked with the authority of a lioness, the power of a goddess, and the wit of an Empress. Heading straight towards me, slowly on her way to devour me. She paused, stopping at the end of my bed. The sway of her hips whispers a deadly promise, the smirk of her red lips hides a great secret. One that she won't tell, but you will discover soon enough. And the smoothness of her voice, brings all down to their knees. Crippling, yet willing to submit to her every request. Biting my lower lip, I could see her in black leather. It hugged her in all of the right places, trying to push her breast out to the point they could just spill over.

Her long hair elegantly pinned up, in a beautiful bun, I bet if she let it out, it'd fall beautiful down her back, adding softness to her strong features. Her dark eyes watching me silently as she began to crawl onto the bed. Her gaze like razors cutting into my soul. Claiming it as hers. I laid on my back, my hands softly drifting up and down my body, only slightly covered by a black oversized t-shirt decorated with a single word in capital red letters, 'OBEY.'

With power, she crawled up until she was positioned right above me. I could almost feel the warmth of her on my face. "What will it be, my kitten?" My bottom lip quivered at the thought. As I pretended and wished her hands were on me. Touching me in ways that only she could. Grasping me and holding me down. But for now, it was my hands that slid slowly over my torso. One, not so gently groped my chest, as the other continued down. My nails scraping my stomach as I neared my core. I needed her, my made-up mistress, to be real, as a dying man needs the afterlife to be. I want to feel her hands brush over my skin, as if I am the most precious life in this world. I crave for her to tie me up, hold me down and take me. Take me with such a force and passion, one would think the world was going to end. My heart throbbed in sadness, just as the dying man's would when he discovers the truth...

Pushing away those thoughts, I closed my eyes, letting my imagination run wild. I wondered what it would be like... If she came in right now, flipped me onto my tummy, hiked up my shirt. And pushed her fingers deep into me. All the while whispering in my ear, telling me that I'm hers. And only ever hers.

I grew wetter as my thoughts progressed. Hotter as I dreamt of her rocking against me, grinding harder and faster. Me screaming and moaning out breathless "Mistress!" as I gush and soak her fingers.

My hand found its way to my increasingly wet slit making a beeline for my rock-hard clitoris. I moaned softly, doing my best to touch gently as to not cum too soon. I pretended that it was her hand, her hand ghosting over me. Which only made me shake all the more.

"Are you ready my little Kitten?" Mmmm... breathing faster now, I pushed down hard on both sides of my clit and rubbed with a passion. My body shocked into overload and began rocking against my fingers. I spread my legs wider, hoping for some stability. But all that mattered at this point was to finish. My core tightened, clit throbbed, and muscles clenched as I neared my sweet release.

So close... Soo... Soo... Close... I moved faster just a little more. My bottom raised off the bed, pushing myself harder onto my slick, wet fingers. So close... but then I stopped dead, just before I even could touch the light of a firecracker orgasm... Because I felt hands resting on my knees... Uh oh.

"By all means cutie, don't stop on my account. I've got a purrrrfect view"

⊠

Chapter 7

# Passion & Poetry-Part 1

I jot my emotions down on a line
Trying to sort through the problems of my life
Trying to make sense of the scars left behind
Trying to find the edge of the lie

But when I look down, all I see
Is the broken me, written in poetry
And with all my passion, I am left in doubt
Trying to summon tears while experiencing a drought

And so, I sit alone, forgotten on the side lines
Looking at the shattered events that created my life
And I am left with this tragic reality
Hidden between the lines of my misguided passion
and unread poetry....

TJ

I'm nervous, I'm also kind of scared, but I will not back down, I won't. Not this time. I looked in my rear-view mirror. I know that I am beautiful, I don't lack self-esteem. Today however, I'm going to do what I've always been reluctant to do. Brushing a strand of my dark brown hair out of the way, I pulled my robe a little tighter on me. I looked into my green eyes and took several deep breaths. 'Ok Stacy, you can do this. No strings, just friends, no problem. Just go in and get it done.' With one final glance I was ready to go. It only took me a few minutes to drive to his house, it looked familiar... The crooked mailbox, the old basketball hoop above the garage. He still lives in the same house he grew up in? That's odd... It was a calming one story, with a nice front yard and big backyard. I slowly approached and parked, the jumping in my stomach managed to triple. I rested my head against the steering wheel.

Perhaps I should enlighten you of my situation. My name is Stacy Montro. And I am a 25-year-old virgin. Not that being a virgin is a bad thing, and trust me, this was all by my own choice. I just decided on my own that I wanted to give it away to a friend... Of course, the guys I've dated lied left and right saying I did everything under the sun with them. But again, I simply couldn't. I found no true desire to go that far with any of them. And the few times I did have the desire to do so, it never felt right enough to follow through. So, I figured why not have my best friend from high school do it? It won't matter if I'm deeply attracted to him or not. He'd know not to hurt me and be kind about it. I can trust him to not rush me, and in the end, I guess it's what I want. So, I called Joseph over the phone, we talked for hours, flirted and laughed. I told him I'd be in town soon and he invited me over to his place for dinner... Well, that's why I'm here now. I shouldn't be doing this... Stepping out of the car I walked to his front door and knocked, waiting impatiently. I know it makes me look easy, but... But it doesn't matter, my mind is made up. I waited a little longer, then rang the doorbell. And waited some more, growing restless, I then did both. What's taking him so long! I rang the doorbell repeatedly now. He did say 5 o'clock... Didn't he? Or maybe I was supposed to come at 7. Dang it, I might be early.

"Dammit! If you ring that annoying bell one more fucking time, I will fu-" The door yanked open revealing a familiar stranger. Joseph's twin sister Tommy J. She stopped in her angry rant and looked shocked to find me standing on the doorstep. I thought this was where Jo lived... Maybe they live together? But that doesn't seem right. Though they are twins, the two looked nothing alike. And didn't ever seem to particularly like each other while growing up. Tommy J was a caramel tan beauty with wavy light brown hair that curled elegantly over her shoulders. Her eyes are a lovely dark chocolate, and almond shaped. She was tall too, 5'10 maybe... She's gotten taller. She has more of a slim, but sturdy boyish figure with strong shoulders. That's not shocking considering all the sports she played throughout our younger years.

She sported a black muscle shirt, and well-loved blue jeans. She's gotten a lot stronger too. Her muscles looked toned and well defined in the light coming from inside. I was just as stunned as she looked. Her pink lips, her strong nose, her thick eyelashes. She always amazed me with her tough, rugged beauty and take no shit attitude. The only thing is, we never got along. Not even a little. She hated me for whatever reason, and made it known. I don't know anyone that had the natural ability to cut someone in half with a single glance like she does.

Her dark eyes roamed over my face and my entire body with an odd look. "Stacy?" She whispered. Wow, I had forgotten about her voice. It always made me feel so... I don't know, just different... Weak maybe? It made me... me desire something. Something so unknown and strange that I could never grasp it. I always thought it was friendship, but that never happened. Her voice, it was raspy, with a musical drift to it. Deep and dark, like a foreboding path that promises something wicked at the end. I could feel the blush creeping to my cheeks. I looked away from her, embarrassed by my own feelings. I always blush when I'm around her. It's the way she looks at me.

"Um, hi TJ. Is Jo here?" I felt like I was in high school all over again. She smiled at me then moved aside. "Would you like to come in?" She asked... Wait, she's inviting me in? That's a first, she used to just close the door in my face when we were younger. Taking a shaky breath, I stepped in. "So, um, how have you been?" She asked, again I gaped at her. Why is she being so nice to me? She's never been nice before. "Oh, I've been good..." I trailed off as she scratched her neck. "Good..." Awkward silence filled the room. I looked at her, her tight shirt showing off her nice body. Well, she definitely has changed at least a bit.

"So, um, where's Jo?" She looked at me, a bit confused as her eyes clouded over. What's with her? "What?" She asked. I rolled my eyes at her. It's like she's lost somewhere. "Jo, your twin brother, the person I'm here to see. Jo, where is he?" I didn't mean to yell at her, but she frustrates me. Add on to that, that I'm nervous, out of my comfort zone and that mother sucker said he'd be here!

Her eyes darkened, and her entire body tensed. I took a step back, I know for a fact that when she gets this way, it always ends with me crying. She never harmed me physically, but her words tend to sting. "Look here Princess, I don't know who the fuckyou think you are, raising your voice at me. But you better put that shit in check unless you want to get your ass spanked!" I cringed back from her, truly afraid. And here I was, thinking I've outgrown my childhood fears. Hahaha... WRONG!!! "Or how 'bout I put that in check, seeing as I've wanted too for so long."

What is she going to do me? Is she going to hit me? Kill me?!? I took another step back as she slowly advanced towards me. "I-I'm s-s-sorry TJ." I could feel the tears swelling, ready to spill over. She had this evil glint in her eyes, one that had the blood rushing from my face. My fear only increased once my back hit the wall. She placed both her hands on the wall on either side of my face. Caging me in. My heartbeat sped up as I looked up at her. She has always been a beautiful fear to me. I wanted nothing to do with her, and now, now she's going to kill me! I closed my eyes praying, in hope of a rescue. Silently waiting for the pain to start, but it didn't come. Instead something warm and soft pushed hard onto my lips. She's.... She's kissing me?!?! I wanted to open my eyes and see if my mind was just being cruel but feared she would realize her mistake and scream at me.

My head began to spin, between my legs tingled. I didn't know a woman, let alone Tommy J could make me feel this. I felt warm, shaky on the inside as her lips caused something to spread throughout my entire body. She kissed with the ease of a professional. This is what it feels like to kiss TJ... this is what it's like to not be in her fire zone. This is amazing. A warm feeling traveled within my body as she pressed herself against me. She was firm, her breasts, her abs. I was held tightly in place, everything around me faded as her tongue traced my bottom lip. She wants in... I cannot pretend I'm not feeling this, wanting this.

Wait... is she gay? I never even thought to ask Jo if she was, but honestly what else could she be? She used to scare the hell out of the boys in school, and the girls. Why is she kissing me?! Why do I like it? Why is it turning me on further than I've ever been turned on before? Am I? That can't be right... Can it? Her hands found their way inside my robe, her fingers gently gliding up along my skin, leaving tingling trails of fire everywhere she touched. I moaned as her fingertips brushed a spot right under my nipple, instantly making it harden. She then pushed her tongue into my mouth. She tasted like sunflowers and French vanilla cream. Her tongue was warm and smooth as it teased my tongue into its game. Oh my... I'm kissing a girl. A woman! And not just anyone, but Tommy freaking J! TOMMY JAY!!! The number one bad ass is frenching me!

But what if Jo walks in? With this thought, dread washed through me. If he sees this, will he speak to me? Of course, Tommy will simply walk away like nothing happened. She'll throw me to the sharks and watch me get eaten alive... I can't hurt him like that. I like this... and for once a small piece of me imagined that she might like me. But, but I can't hurt Jo, he's been nothing but a friend my whole life. Beating up bullies, returning stolen items to me. Being my shoulder to cry on. I can't ruin that. So, I pushed her away from me. Shock was clear on her face, along with lust and now, growing rage. "You shouldn't have done that princess." I ran to the other side of the room facing her. "Please Tommy Jay, we can't do this. I just... I just want to see Jo." She shook her head and looked away, her eyes flashing. "You always wanted him, didn't you? Always looked at him as if he was a fucking God!" What?

"No, I - I don't understand what's going on."

"Huh, that's bullshit Stacy, because only sluts come this far after this long for a fucking booty call..." She paused. "...from an engaged man." He's engaged?!?! She stormed her way towards me. Her body language screaming 'run the hell away!' "I-I didn't know he was engaged!" I cried, following my instincts, I turned and ran. My heart raging in my chest. I can't say that I'm not hurt. I called him, I flirted with him. But he never mentioned even having a girlfriend. I wouldn't have even... she thinks I'm a slut. My eyes burned with tears. I thought he cared about me, I know I haven't seen him in a few years, but he flirted back with me. Telling me he couldn't wait to see me... Th-that he wanted too... Why! Why am I so stupid?

"Stacy!" I kept running. Why am I always so damn emotional around her! Running straight down the hallway I made a sharp left in hopes to see the back door. It only led me to a single door at the end of the hall. Without thinking or looking back, I yanked open the door and closed it behind me, locking it. My heart was racing, my breathing loud. I slumped against the door and took deep breaths. Why didn't he tell me he was engaged? That-that asshole! "'Oh Stacy, I'd love to see you again. Why not come over? We can have dinner, hang out, catch up... God, I bet you're even more beautiful than when I last saw you."'

My chest burned. He's engaged, to be married. He was about to cheat on his fiancé with me. I... I thought he was different, I thought I knew him! But he is just a man like any other man. It's not an excuse, but instead a sad truth. I touched my cheek; it was moist with my tears. Now I understand it... why Tommy is so mad... She probably really does love her brother. And I look like the slut trying to ruin his relationship. She's right, this was a tramp move.

I slowly exhaled, sliding down to the ground. I just want to go home now. My heart hurts, I always remembered Jo to be kind and caring. It's not like I haven't seen him in 10 years... It's only been like 2. He came to my 23rd birthday party, flirted then too. Gave me a beautiful tennis bracelet with green gems. Told me when he saw it, he couldn't help but to get it for me. He's always been nothing but sweet... This, this doesn't seem like him at all. Maybe Tommy is lying, maybe he's not really engaged. I haven't seen Tommy J since High school. But I'm sure she never wanted me around...

Pulling my legs up to my chest, I cried into my knees. I'm not as weak as I look, but this is surfacing a whole lot of demons. At least I'm safe... and she doesn't know where I am.

"OOOH! THE STARS ARE ALL ALINED. WE'VE ONLY GOT THIS TIME. BRIGHTEN UP THE DARK. LET THIS BE THE START!!" Oh god no! The blood drained from my face as my phone blazed to life at full volume. Screaming my beloved song to the point of hatred. Quickly I dug into my purse fumbling to turn that stupid thing off. With an outrageously irregular heartbeat due to stress, I finally was able to achieve my mission. I sighed when the music stopped, and my necessary but highly aggravating phone powered down. Now all I have to do is wait for Jo to get here and I'm free. Then I'm going to probably rip his dick off if he's really engaged. Of all the inconsiderate, arrogant, ill placed, heartless things Jo could have done! Cheat on his fiancé? What a low-

"Staaay-seee" all my hope suffocated and died. The door handle rattled for a second then stopped. Maybe...? "You have five seconds to open this door or you will regret it." Her voice was oddly playful. Like this was a game. I don't feel like it's a game. I feel like I'm being hunted and it's not very fun. She's mad at me, she has a right to be. In her eyes I'm here trying to ruin her brother's soon to be marriage. And she kissed me. W-why'd she kiss me?

I gulped in fear as I got up and backed away from the door, deeper into the dark room. My eyes trained on the eerily silent door. I bumped into something soft, turning around I glided my hand over it. Hum... A bed? A BED! The door swung open, revealing a very angry Tommy Jay with a key in hand. "I-I..." I don't know what to say, she's a ticking time bomb and I don't know how much time I have left. Within a blink of an eye she was in front of me. Rage emitting from her skin like steam. "I told you, you'd regret that."

I ran into a bedroom? Just my luck. There's not supposed to be a room back here! She pushed me back, causing me to fall onto the bed. She then jumped on top of me, I shrank back into the cushion. I don't know what she's going to do, but fear of the unknown shook me in places that only nightmares usually touch. I shook my head back and forth with a growing anxiety. "Tommy please, I didn't know, I'm sorry!" She looked down at me, slowly shaking her head. "I couldn't stop if I wanted too, I have you now. I'm not letting you go." In a romantic novel, that would have almost sounded sweet. But now, it just scares me. I don't understand what she means by that. She never seemed to want me before.

I opened my mouth to speak but she took that as an invitation to kiss me again. For a second, I felt weightless, with her lips against mine. Everything faded once again, leaving only her kiss in its wake. I shouldn't be enjoying this. I should be repulsed, I should be cringing away in disgust and screaming for help. Yet, I can't seem to. Every second her lips push against mine; it lifts me from an invisible jail I didn't know existed. It's as if I'm breathing for the first time. And she is my air. Her hands roughly gripped my sides, while she rocked her lower body onto mine. She was hot on top of me. But she smelled good, inviting even. When did she get between my legs? Why is she so close? A moan slipped from my lips into hers, and a growing wetness now leaked into my favorite lingerie.

I was lost for words. As the realization hit me, yes, she's being rough, and mean. But deep down... I think I like it. Even if I had the strength to tell her to stop, I don't think I could. Because something deep inside of me wants this. And I couldn't say why if asked. Not now that she's trailing kisses down my neck. She grabbed my wrist and pinned them above my head, holding them there with one hand. Her teeth grazing my shoulder. I moaned, shuddering in the exciting naughtiness of it all. I've never felt so alive. So empowered.

With her free hand, she grabbed my robe and tore it open. Revealing my emerald green, thin lacey lingerie, and nothing else. And that quickly, the warmth she was emitting, turned to ice. She sneered at me, her cold eyes cutting me in half, like I said, no one does it like she does. "You fucking whore, you really came here just to fuck him! All these years and you're still blind, still fucking ignorant of what's right in your fucking face! They said you were a slut, but I..." Her voice broke, the weight of her words pulled me down and under. She stopped speaking and looked away from me. "I guess I was wrong about you... I guess it doesn't matter anymore." Her hands tightened on my wrist. She closed her eyes, her grip getting tighter and tighter, my wrists were starting to burn.

But that hurt so little in comparison, as my heart broke in two, then crumbled to the ground. Is that what she thought of me the whole time? All I ever wanted was something other than hatred from her. I always looked up to her, even as she looked down on me. But she's right, just as she's always been right about me. I'm no better than a slut, I did call him for sex. I sniffled, squeezing my eyes shut. "You have no right to cry Stacy... You have no idea what you've put me through." I opened my eyes and looked up into hers. Her eyes were red and even in the little light coming in from the hallway, I could see the shining of tears. She shook her head. "I just can't right now." She sighed and rolled off of me, sitting up on the bed. For a second, I just laid there, shocked, even as my mind tried to bring me back to my previous thought process. She said she was wrong about me... not right. I, I wonder what she meant. I slowly sat up, rubbing my sore wrist. "Tommy?" She turned her head away from me.

"Like the ghost of love
To a lover's dream
She came to me
Out of the sea

And though I fought
To make her go
She surfaces
When I'm alone

Her grace, her power
Her voice, her sway
She's a blinding beauty
Yet, deliverer of pain

And once she's gotten
Within my heart
She tears it out
She shreds it apart

She lulled me in
With deep green eyes
A shallow kiss
A hastily goodbye

A shattered heart
A broken spirit
She awakened me

And then she feared it

She runs away
While she cries
I'm her monster
She, my Frankenstein

But in the end
I am the fool
Who fell in love
With a deceitful pool

Back to the sea
She will return
She'll eat my pain
As I have learned

She's a ghost
Just a haunting dream
A figment of love
That came out of the sea

She captured me
She filled me whole
Then called me out
To the sea, I'd go

But her Sirens call
Both tempting and sweet
Fades away
the further I reach

And so I'll drown
While she swims away
Reaching for her
Praying to be saved

And in the end
I am the fool
Who wished for love

On a dinky pool

And so the taste
Is on my lip
Like the broken memory
Of our tragic kiss

As she feeds
Upon my heart
I have nothing left ...
She's tearing me apart..."

She whispered softly. My heart squeezed painfully in my chest. "That was... It was..." I was lost for words. It doesn't make sense, but if it's about me... It paints me out to be the really bad guy. "JUST GO!" She yelled, I jumped back in fear. Tears shining in her brown eyes. "Please, just leave me alone Stacy. You're good at that, you know? And you're really good at being the victim. Forgetting anything that makes you look bad. So please, go home. Forget about me like you always do and pretend that you're the only one ever hurt. Leave me to my evilness, because you obviously see me as nothing else. You only have an interest in fucking my brother, so fuck him. Like hell if I care what you do... I won't care anymore. I don't want you." Her voice was thick, as tears spilled out of her eyes. She made no effort to conceal them... I don't understand what I've done. She's the one who ran me down. Held me against her bed and kissed me. How am I the bad guy? Forget it, she's crazy. I slowly stood up, holding my robe tightly in my hands, fearful of her exploding again. It was as if light fled from her, running from her just like I always did. Wait... I don't pretend that I'm the victim, never do I act weak and helpless. She just scares me, she's always scared me, so I run. That's not pretending, that's just fear. But... But.

"Leave" she said, standing up and turning away from me. Her shoulders hunched a bit. Her body shook slightly with her silent cries. And in that moment, she was no longer my predator. Instead, I was the mouse that pricked the elephant. "Just leave...." She whispered; her beautiful voice slurred with tears. "...go" I stood straight, my heart pounding. A part of me wanted to run, jump in my car and forget this ever happened... But I can't leave like this. Why? Why am I finding it difficult to leave? This could be a play; she could be plotting my downfall. Yet, a part of me refused to see it. I couldn't find it in me to turn away. I've never seen her cry before, and a place within me wanted her to be strong again, even as I feared it.

"No" I said, my voice steady, even as I shook within. She slowly turned; her eyes blazed with fire. It made my heart stop, and my mind instantly telling my heart 'I told you so.'

"What?" She hissed. I took a deep breath. Squaring my shoulders. Feeling like a soldier readying for war.

"No. I'm not leaving Tomm-" She ran at me, pushing me hard against the wall. Pinning me there. "What the hell is wrong with you?" I screamed at her. Feeling emotionally and physically hurt. I'll have bruises all over my back now. "All I want is for you to leave. And the one thing I want from you, you never want to give! Why are you so damn stubborn? What? You think that because you saw a soft side of me, now you can save me? I don't need your fucking delusional heroism! I need you to go. I need you to walk your stick up the ass self, right on out of my life. You're not a fucking princess, I'm not your friend, I'm not your knight. I'm obviously nothing to you, and never was, so just leave me alone! Or I swear I will do something to you and really show you how bad this bully can be."

She leaned in closer, murder in her eyes. I don't understand her, she's so unstable. And had always had it out for me for no reason. For once, I won't let her take her issues out on me. I puffed up my chest and started screaming the things I've been holding in for so long. I let it out in a flash of anger and misunderstood desire to be more than a hated target for her. "What did I do to make you hate me? All I've ever been is afraid of you, ever since I first met you! You've caused nothing but terror in me, and no matter what I did, you hated me. You've never done anything, and I mean absolutely nothing to make me see you as anything more than a scary bitch and an unforgiving, arrogant, selfish, immoral bully!"

Tommy stopped, she stepped back, releasing me from her hold and shook her head. Wow, did that really work? If I had known it was that easy to turn off her angry mode, I'd have done it a lot sooner. "Really?" She asked, with an alarming lack of emotion in her voice. As if she were turning to stone. "You're a lair Stacy."

"What?" I asked, shocked. Did she really just call me a lair? She stepped back, shaking her head.

"I said, 'You're a fucking lair.' Do you even remember when we first met?" She asked as she turned away from me, her voice softer... I nodded, then spoke up. "Fourth grade... I think."

"Yeah... Joseph and I were turning nine. And our mom invited this new kid to our party because it was just her and her mother. New to the neighborhood too..." I watched her but could barely remember the time she was speaking of.

"We were playing hide and seek, and... And I later found out that Joseph had told her that if she finds the birthday boy, she had to kiss him happy birthday. She got tagged it. And She found me, hiding behind the big tree... I... I should have climbed it, but I didn't. I should have, then none of this would have happened. But I didn't. I didn't." She trailed off, as if lost in thought. Maybe a part of her regretted that lack of action. How can something like that be so important to her? Her fist clenched, she continued.

"She found me, asked me my name. I said, 'Tommy and it's my birthday', and she... She told me I was beautiful... And then she kissed me. Her lips touched mine and awoke something in me. The way it felt, the power it had. Nothing felt more right, more perfect, more shocking to my system... My first kiss was by this beautiful green-eyed new girl. Who's name I didn't even know... You kissed me." My mouth hung open as the shattered memory started to surface. "You kissed me and made my heart jump. My palms itch. My eyes close. You kissed me. Then smiled. I said 'Hi, I'm Joseph's sister...' And before I could get another word out. Before I could ask your name, or even offer a hug. You looked at me as if I were cursed. You spat on the ground, wiping the taste of me from your lips and ran away crying. As if I had hurt you. You ran to your mom, begging her to take you home, completely hysterical. Your mom took you home. I ran after you, trying to calm you down. But all anyone saw was that weird girl Tommy, chasing after the sweet new girl. I was sent to my room without presents, cake, or even a hug... Because I scared the new girl. I learned a lesson that day, as my brother opened our presents. No one will believe the freak over the angel. And that in the end, only the normal people win."

I gasped... I don't remember that at all! I closed my eyes and felt them burning as tears washed down my cheeks. The memory, though hazy, flooded back. Me running to my mom, crying. Begging her to take me home. I was scared, I remembered that very well. I was terrified. But, I... I was... "Tommy?"

She faced me. "I'm really trying not to do something I'll regret. Leave, you have nothing here. No need to try and prove anything. Just leave." My heart broke. It's the realization that I am no better than my mother. I kissed a fresh-faced kid when I was no older, then blamed her. "I always wanted you to like me" I whispered.

"No you didn't."

"Well, I did... I was only a child." She laughed without humor.

"You don't even remember it." I bit my lip. "Tommy, I was only eight." She angrily snapped at me, pushing me against the wall again.

"I WAS ONLY EIGHT TOO!" She punched the wall near my head. I jumped, shaking in fear. "You always find excuses and reasons for your actions. If all you ever wanted was my friendship, then why in the fuck did you avoid me that entire summer! Huh? Why, when I came to your house to apologize for something I didn't even do, you told your mom that you didn't want to see me? Why, when I tried, and tried, and tried, you found time to be with Joseph... But wouldn't step ten feet near me? Why did you continuously punish me, for something you did to me? Why!"

Tears continued to fall from her eyes. In all my life, I have never known Tommy J to cry, yet now they fell freely. Unleashing quaking emotions within my soul. And I realized that my answer was as simple as the emotion I've always felt...

"Fear" I whispered, looking down at the floor. My eyes filled with tears as I glanced timidly up at her, her cheeks inflamed with raw emotions. And she looked away from me. It's my turn to speak. "All I ever heard from my mother when it came to Gays and Lesbians were that they were going to hell. They were filthy heathens that held no respect or reason. To fear them from turning me into one of them or I'd lose her love. And I'm sorry okay? I'm sorry that I was terrified that I kissed a girl. I'm sorry that even though I liked it, I ran. I'm sorry that I was so afraid I blocked it out and hurt you." I began to sob. "I'm sorry I wasn't as strong as you Tommy, and I'm sorry you hate me... That you've always hated me..."

I covered my eyes. It makes perfect sense now. Why I couldn't stand dating a guy for more than three dates. Why I can't stomach the idea of having sex. Why I was so obsessed with Tommy but could never understand why. I felt disgusted with myself. I never even thought that I might like women. Or that I might have caused such harm to the girl I wanted to love... No, I don't love her... but I do... have... attraction? Oh my God! I've always been attracted to her! It was attraction?!? No, No, No! Yes? Why!

"I don't hate you Stacy." Her voice pulled me out of my inner battle with my ugly truths. Wait, what'd she say? "I've never hated you. Being so angry to the point of wanting to harm you emotionally, like you've hurt me... yes. But I couldn't hate you." She turned away and sat on the edge of her bed. "I did everything in my power to make sure you were happy." She whispered.

That honestly enraged me. She's been nothing but a menace to me my entire life. Never offering a single word of kindness my way. "Now who's the lair Tommy? You've only ever made my childhood hell." She looked at me, her eyes looking somewhat lost. I stuck my chin out, feeling brave and continued on. "Joseph was the one who made me smile and kept me safe. You were always the bully. As if I'd believe that you tried at all. In fact, you could be lying right now. Just messing with me like you used to do. Joseph probably isn't engaged at all, you're a lair." I felt a sick sense of glee at being one up one her. It's just wrong that she'd lie like that. But what would you expect from a bully?

She laughed, it was full and beautiful, just like her voice. But also, unsettling and seductive just like her presence. "Jo never did a single damn thing for you, other than take credit." Err, what? She stood up, facing me. "Do you really think it was him? All that time? All those years? He, my soft hands brother Jo?" She took a step closer. My back hit the wall as I attempted to take one step back. "I was the one fighting off your bullies, I was the one who returned anything anyone stole from you and placed it in your locker. I used to put gifts in your locker on your birthday, or after Christmas... In fact, every holiday you were given a gift from me. And I beat the living shit out of any guy who bragged about what you two may or may not have done. I chose to believe that they were lying, that somewhere deep in you..." She stopped, took a deep breath, and continued. "I spent my evenings making sure you got home safe, and my free time thinking of ways to make you smile. But none of it ever mattered, because Jo always got the credit. And eventually I convinced myself that it didn't matter that you were with him, or with any guy... As long as you were happy and safe." My mouth hung open. Did she... Did she really feel that way about me?

No, no no no. She has to be lying... But is she? I want to say she is; I really do... But I can't deny the fact that her side makes sense. The things I used to fluff off when it came to certain things, were now floating to the surface. How when I would find a gift in my locker, instead of saying 'I knew you'd love the opal earrings'. He'd say, 'I knew you'd like it'. Or when I got news that someone beat up Jack Vent after he said I gave him a blow job and that I'm a dirty whore. Jo simply replied 'Well, I can't let him call you names'. He always gave me generic answers. Then rushed to a different subject. I never questioned it, just thinking him to be modest. It was a flaw in my own innocent belief that he was honest, and I shouldn't question his kindness.

That... That fucking jerk! I, I can't believe he'd do that. But, but I can. I'm going to kick his sorry pathetic ass. I'm going to rip him a new one, that lying sack of shit! He's a fucking fucker, that fucker! I was fuming. He took credit on all of it. Was anything I've ever gotten from him even real? I want to fucking kill him. I feel so embarrassed, so ashamed. All this time, after all these years, he's been secretly laughing at me. While his own sister worked her ass off. He's a snake! A slimy slithering predator. No higher than the dirt he crawls on! Argh!!! Full of anger, I looked up at her. As my rage increased, so did my sorrow. All these years, it was her. And I never saw it, he never let me see it. Never once mentioned that it was his sister. How could she stand him, because I'm rapidly finding him to be insufferable.

She stood in front of me now. Her hand on my waist. "He never loved you the way I did Stacy. And I hope you believe that." She bent down and kissed my forehead. It's the nicest she's ever been to me. And in a way, it hurt more than her anger. It was as if she were letting me go, and the fear came right back. She took a step back, shaking her head. "I've always wanted to say something to you. To grab you and hold you and confess it all..." She ran her fingers through her hair. Her eyes full of sadness. "But it didn't matter. You were stuck on him like glue. Every word he said, everything he did. I knew I couldn't be anything but a mistake in your eyes. And so, I was angry. Always mad when I saw you with him..." My heart squeezed painfully in my chest.

The light has been turned on; the darkness revealed. I felt like kicking myself, everything I knew to be true about this set of twins was lies. Roles reversed, switched. I bowed my head in shame. I've obsessed over TJ all throughout middle school, and high school. Always watched her from the corner of my eyes. Thinking that the sweating in my palms, and the dryness of my mouth was nothing but fear, and fear alone. But I may have been wrong. Is it possible that even then, I was attracted to her? That I was drawn to her bold smirk, her cunning gaze, her seductive voice? That I may have dreamed of us holding hands, and her looking at me with something other than hatred and anger. That...that this time I'm the one in the wrong?

The silence grew and I was unsure of what to do, what to say even. Eventually she shook her head and looked at me through her eyelashes. She exhaled deeply, taking another step back. "It's obvious that you don't want to leave, so I will. Joseph should be here in an hour or so. Have fun." She walked out of the door. Leaving me bare.

☒

Chapter 8

# Passion & Poetry-Part 2

She walked passed me, leaving me cold. "Tommy..." I reached out, taking her arm. "Please" I whispered. "Please what?" She wasn't looking at me. "Don't go" I'll beg if I have to... I just can't let it end like this, I just can't. She sighed heavily, still looking away. Her shoulders square. "I just... I just can't right now Stacy" She whispered.

"Well then don't!" I yelled. "Who's playing victim now, huh? You could have, at any point, confronted me. Told me the truth. But instead you let your brother take all the credit. Here I was, thinking that you were the strongest person I've ever known, and you couldn't even do that!" She slowly turned around. "Would you have believed me Stacy? Had I come to you, confessed my truths, would you have even for a second, believed me?"

"Well, yes" I said, even in uncertainty. "Don't fool yourself. I'm the bad guy remember? I'm the freak. I'm the weirdo without a heart, the indecent twin. The abnormal offspring of anger and filth. Or was I mistaken, that it wasn't you and Jo saying those things? It's easy to believe the worst about a bully Stacy. What's one lie? What's one truth? But you? You could do no wrong. I don't understand why you're fighting so hard for me to believe in you. I've lost my faith in you long ago, little girl. No use in trying to bring it back."

I became silent, mute even. I never knew that she could hear us giggling from a closed door down the hall. And, and... and I have no words. I did say those things. And frankly, she was evil to me. My words were the only power I had against her. And it made me feel strong, even as it made me sour. "What did you expect from me Tommy? You terrified me... You made me question everything about myself. You made me so damn nervous around you, and yes, in my eyes you were the ultimate evil. And even now, you're toying with me. You're hot, then you're cold. You're angry, and then you're sad. I don't know what to take from this because I'm continuously the one accused. I know I was rotten to you from closed doors. But-but you were evil to me face to face..." I took a deep breath, sliding my robe back onto my shoulders. Anger made my heart race and hands shake.

"Do you remember the dance in seventh grade?" I asked. "Well? Do you?" I spat at her. Her fist clenched again.

"How could I forget it Stacy... That's the night you first kissed him. He never shut up about it. He went on and on for months..."

"Oh... Yeah, that did happen. I completely forgot about that... But the thing I remember, was going into the bathroom, and you were in there. In your worn blue jeans. A black, sleeveless undershirt, tucked in. And a Jean jacket on top. Your hair was pulled back into a ponytail. You were leaning against the wall... Watching me when I came in..." The memory took center stage in my mind. Reminding me of that moment. The moment her eyes captured me. And refused to let me go. How I got lost in their deathly gaze, it lacked warmth, lacked kindness... but a fire blazing hotter than the sun burned within them. And stole my breath away. "You watched me, then started walking. I didn't know what to do, other than just watch you back. You stood in front of me. And... and... and you said 'You look beautiful tonight Stacy... If only they knew what I know... Then little miss popular would come crashing down. You'd be nothing more than an unwanted freak, just like the rest of us. But who am I to let your dirty secret slip? I'll keep your secret, Miss Privileged. But be warned, my niceness is running thin."'

A smile played on her lips as she faced me. "I'm surprised, you remember that." She said somewhat amused. Why the heck is she amused? That confused and terrified me! I had no idea what she was talking about. I thought she had serious dirt on me. Like my secret collection of Bratz dolls and stickers. "I remember it because you're a fucking roller-coaster!" I screamed stepping towards her. She became very serious, very quickly. "You went from compliment, to threat faster than a heart changes beat. That night haunted me, you... You fucking freak!" And then it slipped out. It fell from my angry lips faster than I could stop it. And instant regret boiled like bile in my stomach. "Tommy... I didn't mea-"

"Stop" was all she said. Her hand coming up, silencing me like a queen to her subject. Her eyes roaming over me seemingly lifeless. "Freak," she licked her lips, as I mentally kicked myself repeatedly. She just, she gets under my skin! "Yeah, that sounds about right. I'm the freak. Well, congratulations on being rotten face to face for the first time. Do you feel better now? Liberated even? How long have you kept it in? Huh, little girl? All your fucking life!?"

"Oh, I'm sorry princess, it must be so hard fitting in. Entirely unfair to be instantly accepted and loved by everyone. It's just so easy not to be the fucking freak! Well, cheers to you for finally letting it all out, cause I'm sure that dirty laundry was reeking up a storm." Her sarcasm was painful... But not nearly as much as the poison behind it. I gritted my teeth closed. Anger casting a red haze on everything. And my mouth opened before reason and logic had time to keep it shut.

"At least I wasn't the coward who was too afraid to be who I was. I understand that something traumatic happened to me, and that I blocked it out. But what's your excuse Tommy? Too weak to state the truth? Left to act like a second-grade school boy, hurting a girl that you liked. Who's the weak one here? Because one of us knew the truth and it sure as hell wasn't me. You're nothing but a coward." I seethed at her, my words shooting out like daggers. "You're just as weak as Jo. You cry because he took the credit, well then you shouldn't have given him the pass. Miss 'I'm too damn emotional to confront myself'. Your laundry is just as dirty as mine. But at least now that I know I have it, I have the decency to air it."

Her eyes flashed with rage. And I stood my ground. "You know what TJ? Thank you, because now I understand a whole lot of things about me that I was completely unaware of. So, I'm going to go on with my life. Because as you've said, I obviously have nothing left here. I'm done, and I'm going." I picked up my purse off the ground and walked passed her. Her scent brushed my nose, her sweet taste lingered on my lips. Her fire breathed within my chest. But regardless, I don't know her. And she wants nothing more than to hate me. Her rage, firing from the outside, mine lurking within. Lesson learned. At least I now understand the meaning behind my behavior, why my eyes wander. Why I find no desire in the many men I've dated.

She... She makes me feel desire, and passion, and pain, and a tidal wave of uncontrollable and unquenched emotions. Now the pressing desire to leave this house and flee from her, pushed me forward... This house, I've played in this house for many years, I've spoken to the walls, and hid inside the closets. I've climbed the trees and helped cleaned the tile floors... tiles. Hardwood? I looked down at the mahogany floors that shinned up at me. Causing reality to be questioned. In fact, the last door on the left should have been the out door to the side of the house. I know this because I've ran out of it many times. Finding my way, away from the fighting twins and heavy atmosphere. I would often fly down the hall in tears after Tommy let loose her hurtful words and run home. But now... there's a room there?

"You're not going anywhere Stacy" she snapped me out of my confusion and pulled me back. "Let go of me. And what happened to the house? Why is it all turned around?" Her anger defused as she stared at me. "I... I'm remodeling it" I looked back down at the floors. "You mean, you're having it remodeled, right?" I asked, happy for a lighter subject. "No, I'm remodeling it. I own this house now. And am doing all the work on it" I looked up at her, stunned. I didn't know she was handy. I shouldn't be surprised that I didn't know, I mean, I'm seriously finding out that I'm a terribly poor judge of character.

Nervously, I looked down at her hand that continued to hold my arm in its hard grasp. Warmth spread up, warming my cheeks. "It looks good Tommy..." I glanced at her, then looked away quickly when my eyes met her piercing gaze. "What the hell is with you Stacy? You called me hot and cold, but I honestly don't know whether to push you out... Or down. What game are you playing with me?" She let go of me and I faced her, my anger blazing again. Dammit if she doesn't make me feel hormonal!

"What? I'm not playing a game. I tried to leave, and you keep pulling me back. As if you actually want me to stay! Then you get mad at me as if it's my fault. If you'd just keep yourself together, then I'll be on my merry fucking way! You're freaking unstable, there's something wrong with you and blaming me won't fix you!" Okay... I snapped; I did. I should apologize. But I won't, she's crazy... did she just say she'd hold me down? That's crazy! Right? Right! My mouth went dry, my palms itched. So, why do I appear to like that idea? Maybe because when she did it earlier... It was fun, even as it was terrifying.

She growled at me. Fearful, I took a step back. "17 years Stacy. Why? Why on earth would I fucking want you to stay? What the fuck do you do to me? The first fucking moment that I was finally free of all the fucking pain you've caused me, you show up at my door! Every time I think I'm passed you! You show the fuck up in my damn life. You're like a curse, wrapped in a blessing that I can't touch. You're a cure to the disease you carry. You're a vixen, a siren, the physical representation of a walking fucking disaster! You break me every, single, fucking time! You pull me in and shred me. And by a fucking hex, laid by you! I can't seem to kill what you've put inside me! You!...

"Why do I want you to stay?!"

Her words slammed into me. Blasting one painful slap after another. And even as it hurt, and stung, it was beautiful in its own disfunction. I bowed my head, tears falling. "You're not the only one hurt Tommy... You're not the only one who has feelings. You feel cheated? I feel used. You and your brother played me like a harp. One laughed, the other cried. And you watched me, for 17 years. And no, I'm not certain if you had stepped up, that I would have believed you. But you didn't even try, you just watched... you..." I trailed off, still looking down.

I'm not sure how to handle my emotions. It was nothing but a game for one... And a tragedy for the other. This is not what I wanted. This... This isn't me. Even if I like her, I just can't do this. I can't be with her and do this. This is dangerous. I stepped back, my heart painfully gripping in my chest. I liked the way she kissed, liked the way her hands gripped me. But I'm a toxin to her. And I never even took the time to know her. And the one I thought I knew... I didn't know at all. I turned away from her, all out of words. All out of reasons. I shouldn't have ever come; I should have listened to that voice inside and kept driving. I shook my head and turn to leave.

"Camp Wichita. Sixth grade" she spoke. I stopped moving. My back to her. "What about it?" I felt tired, drained even. "We were assigned to the same cabin. As well as your friend Rachel. That first night... you didn't sleep at all. You had nightmares all night in fear because my brother took you to go see Jason X and you were terrified that the camp counselors were going to kill us all." I closed my eyes. Remembering that first night. I was so tired the next day, I could barely do any of the activities. "Yeah... I remember that," but then the nightmares all stopped.

"The next night..." I felt her hand gently lay on my shoulder. "That night, as you were tossing and turning. I got up out of bed. You were crying in your sleep, begging them not to kill you. I shook your shoulders until you woke up. It's the one time I had the courage. The strength to do what my heart told me I should. You were disoriented. But I climbed into your bunk and spooned you. Talking to you until you fell back asleep... and you mumbled a thank you... to Rachel."

Oh... my heart squeezed painfully yet again. I gave all her credit away too. She slowly turned me around, forcing me to face her. "In that moment I realized that it didn't matter. Whether or not I got credit for helping you. Because I wanted you safe and happy by any means necessary. So, every night, I'd stay up, almost hoping for the dreams to return. Just so I'd have a reason to climb into your bed. Hold you tight. And protect you from your unseen monsters. Because in a way... " she looked away, her hair falling into her eyes. "...you were protecting me from mine."

I looked up at her, wide eyed. She is like an unsolved mystery. A few tears shined on her golden cheeks. She's the one. Every morning I woke up alone. Knowing that someone was there. I always assumed it was Rachel. But I am continuously wrong. Her hands still rested on my shoulders. I slowly reached up and touched her cheek. Her dark, chocolate eyes moved and locked with mine. Those eyes have captivated me my entire life. Erupting me from the inside out. They invade my dreams, they pull me in, even as they repel me. Her lips parted; her eyes dilated. Her caramel cheeks flushed. I could end this. I could leave. I should leave. I should run out and never look back. I know I should, everything in me tells me I need to. But I just can't walk away from her. I don't think I want to.

"No" she said, glaring me down. "No?" why is she saying no? She pushed me back against the wall. Not hard, but forceful. "You're not running away from me again. Not this time Stacy. Hell will freeze over." And her lips slammed against mine. My heart shot into my throat as her passion froze me in place. I was drowning and she, the ocean wanting my life. With a fire, her lips rushed against mine, making me crave the darkest things. Her darkness, her raw energy, her burning kisses and strong hands, which held me where I stood, even as my legs grew weak.

I can't breathe, I don't want to. Her lips were soft, yet strong. The warmth of her breath filled me. I found no desire to stop her. The only thing coursing through my mind was the uncontrollable drive to push forward. To kiss her back. To have more as my body ached for something I've never experienced. I pushed my lips against hers. Feeling both the pain of my youth, and the unspoken attraction for my captor.

My arms locked around her neck, her hands almost painfully gripping my waist. Never have I ever wanted something so bad, so urgently. And to have her look at me with something other than disdain. Anything other than passiveness. And now, now her tongue is grazing my bottom lip, asking for entrance. I didn't tell my lips to part for her. But they did... Anything she asked of me at this point, I wouldn't be able to refuse. Only to respond in a way that might bring about the most pleasure.

And though a part of me, rearing its ugly head, whispered that she may hit it then quit it. I pushed it away. Locking it out. I only want her. Only need her. Even if just in this moment. My fingers tangled in her hair. My lungs burning for the lack of oxygen, her body pressed tightly against mine. It excited my skin and thrilled my being. I am lost to her. Her tongue played a game with mine, tempting it out of my mouth and into hers. She watched me with a powerful gaze as she gently sucked the length of my tongue. My clit exploded to life, throbbing between my clenched thighs. My heart racing and mind spinning. I can't believe this is happening, this is unreal! This is the most pleasure I have felt in my entire life. My childhood fear, my secret longing. The woman who captivated and terrified me.

A moan broke from my parted lips, as she roughly hiked my leg over her hip. A growl rumbling from her chest. The warmth from her core seeped through my thin undies. Causing my own body to shiver in lust. Clear as day now, crystal even. Her lips fought mine in a power struggle, she overwhelmed me easily, but I hung onto her. Even as her hips moved against mine, and as her hands traveled down, gripping my outer thighs. I felt the ground leave me as she picked me up, pinning me between her and the wall. A fire burned at my core, throbbing parts of me that has only ever been active in private. Again, a growl rumbled out of her, her piercing eyes stealing my air away. "You always make me crave you. Why? Why do I want you naked so bad? What is it that you do to me?"

I blushed, unable to look away. "I-I-I" her lips locked with mine, effectively shutting off my mumbling. She wrapped my legs around her and hooked her hands under my ass. I always knew she was strong, but this... but I... My mind went blank as she dropped me onto a bed. Before I could even comprehend more about it, she was on top of me. Her eyes stared me down, her lips red and parted. Was she craving me as much as I crave her? Apparently, because her eyes roamed over me with the hunger of a lioness, as her tongue sensually licked her upper then bottom lip. Ending it in a bite. As if savoring the taste of me. Me? I wanted to ask why me? But my questions fell away as she slowly brushed her lips against mine. Does she feel my insecurity, can she tell? I don't know, but her fire seemed to calm as she looked down at me. Causing my heart to go wild. Lifting up, she grabbed my arms and gently pinned them above my head. I'm not ignorant when it comes to sex, but I am completely unknowledgeable as to what it is that two women do. I just... Other than touching myself every now and then. I... I mean, Lesbian sex is like uncharted territory. But I have a feeling that I'm about to learn a few key pointers right now.

Her body gently rocked against mine, my legs parted involuntarily for her. All on their own accord, it seems. I'm too lost to actually control my body functions. Her warm kisses pulled me back to her as she slid between my thighs. The heat of her body made the pressure below only intensify. Where is my relief?!? I feel like I'm suffocating, but at the same time, I don't want to breathe. That evil voice in the back of my mind told me I should stop. Why would I want to? As if reading my inner thoughts, she spoke against my neck.

"Don't fight this Stacy, not again. Feel me" she released one of my hands, brought it down and pressed it against her chest. Her heartbeat was strong and pounding against my palm. Her nipple was hard, pressed against the fabric of her shirt. Her breast was soft and warm, touching it tickled my palm and ignited my imagination. Her hips jerked forward with a fresh wave of wanting, rubbing against my need. I gasped for air as the mixture of pleasure and the uncontrollable ache between, throbbed throughout my body. She pulled my hand back up, locked it in place once again. My skin was hot, her body, on top of mine, was even hotter. I don't want her to stop. It would shatter me if she did. She didn't, instead her teeth grazed my shoulder. I pulled against her grasp. But she held onto my wrist relentlessly, caging me underneath her. Her grip only getting tighter the more I pulled. It hurt, but the pain was instantly drowned out when her knee pressed up against my damp crotch. I moaned out, my eyes tightly closed. "Do you want this Stacy? Do you need this?" Yes! I nodded my head, trying to breathe again. "Tell me" she whispered into my ear. My core clenched and throbbed, my legs shaking. Her knee still pressed against me. Tempting me forward in the most exotic way. I rocked my hips to help relieve the tension, but she simply pulled her leg back just enough to barely brush against. A strangled cry jumped out of me as I tried harder to create the friction I desperately desired.

Her grip tightened even harder as I tried to free my wrist. "Tell me!" this time she growled. "Yes" I whispered, "I-I do" she leaned down, her lips only inches from mine. Her warm breath fanned over my face. She smells wonderful, she always has. "Louder" was all she said, her eyes dilated as she watched me. I stared up at her confused even as I seemed to rock my hips against air. She growled when nothing came from my lips. "I want you to beg, I want you to admit that you want me as much as I've wanted you. I want you to scream it..." Her knee pressed into my crotch, sending sparks into my brain. "...beg me to do things to you. Give me consent, give me permission."

I moaned and closed my eyes tightly. "Please Tommy..." my voice shook as the words fumbled from my lips. Words I never thought I'd say. Words, that I can never unspeak. "I want you to take me, please take me." She leaned down, my wrist still in her grasp. Her knee rubbing lightly on my damp core. Taking one hand away but managing to still keep a hold of my wrists, her free hand cupped my place. Causing everything in me to shutter in need. "You're so wet for me Stacy. But I don't think you were quite loud enough. I don't think everyone heard you yet. So, try again" I can't believe her! But at the same time, her fingers were pressing the silk fabric of my underwear into my folds, making them wetter. "Tommy please!" I said louder, even as my cheeks flamed red. I felt her fingers rub the outside of my panties. Applying pressure onto my throbbing nub. My hips jerked forward, no longer thinking of my actions. "Is it mine to take?" She whispered in my ear, licking up my neck. She added more pressure to my core then started to circle my clit. "Is it?!" her passionate voice raised. I nodded vigorously, lust and want taking over me.

She moved her hand, sliding her fingers under the waistline of my underwear. My entire body shook, my toes curled. Fire burned within my core as her fingers ghostly touched my clit. "Fuck!" I squeezed my eyes shut, my body writhing in shock. "That's it, I like when you tell me how you really feel." Her melodic voice pushed me to the edge. I felt on the brink of naughty, on the verge of dirty, and on the cusp of bliss. As the words shot from my mouth before my mind had time to stop them. "I want you to fuck me Tommy!" I yelled, with need and desire. Never have I ever imagined those words would leave my lips. Never have I wanted them to, until now. Her warm breath fanned my face. "Perfect" and her finger slammed into me. She stuck one seemingly thick finger in. I moaned out, arching my back. Slowly, she pushed it in and out. I clenched around her, she's so strong, this feels so good.

I've never been penetrated before, yet her finger filled me with both pain and joy. As she slid deeper into me. Breathing heavily into my ear, her lips latched onto my neck, I'm positive a bruise will appear. Then she trailed wanting kisses over my shoulder and the swell of my breast. I could feel her finger going knuckle deep into me. I whimpered and tried to move away from her as the pain increased. Stretching me and becoming uncomfortable. But I found myself locked in place within her strong arms. She was stretching me open and rubbing against my walls. My hips moved against her finger, filling me up and pulling me closer to the peak of pleasure. As I tried to breathe past the pain. "Damn you're tight. Fuck, baby." I couldn't help the smile that broke my face in two. She called me baby. She continued to push her finger into me. After a bit of time, I grew accustomed to the digital invasion. And the pleasure started to outweigh the pain. My hips began to rock against her finger. Inviting it in with each stroke. And clenching tightly when she pulled out. The gentle roughness of her finger was exciting. Definitely the hands of a woman who works for a living. "Damn" she moaned again, pushing in faster and harder. Wetness flooded from me as she did oddly wonderful things with her tongue on my neck. She lifted up slightly, her eyes were lit with lust. Her lips red. She's sexy, and she always has been.

"Now, I'm going to feast on you." I wasn't sure if she meant it literally or rhetorically... But her finger left me, causing me to immediately protest. And in one swift motion, she slipped my undies clean off. Then immediately started playing with my hardened pearl as she watched me. Slowly, she crept down my body, her eyes trained on me. I felt my heart in my throat, my entire body tense and waiting. A fire lit in her eyes, and before I could question it, she grabbed ahold of my knees and forced them up, shamelessly exposing me. I tried to resist her, for what reason? I'm not really sure. She bit her bottom lip eyeing me like candy. "You gonna resist me Princess? Are you going to say no?" As she spoke, her finger ghosted over my clit, sending shocks of pleasure through me. This made my hips jump, and legs spread open. I hissed, "What was that? I didn't quite hear you Stace." She spread my lips open, blowing cool air against my opening.

"Fuuuuck" I moaned breathlessly.

"With pleasure." A feeling unlike one I have ever experienced washed over me as I felt something soft flick against my clit. "Oh shit! Fuck!" My body jolted; my chest burned. The fuck is she doing to me? My head slammed back against the bed as her tongue tortured me slowly. I never knew something so vital could tear me down so quickly. Shaking under the weight of the pleasure she was forcing on me, I couldn't think, unaware if I was breathing or not. But I couldn't find an ounce of restraint to care. Every lick tore away at the fabrication of understanding I thought I had. So easily were my defenses stripped from me, I question if they were ever there.

Her tongue was warm, it softly tickled the hardened tip of my clit. My tongue stuck to the roof of my mouth, everything falling out of focus around me. Her lips closed around my clit, sealing it within her mouth. My hands shot forward and tangled into her soft hair. Then without warning, she slammed her finger back into me. I moaned out loudly, pulling hard against her.

"That's it baby, I want you to lose control." Funny, here I was thinking it was already gone. Her voice was rough, her cheeks flushed, her lips wet with my own liquid. Why is that a turn on? I'm so freaking confused right now! She pushed her finger deeper in me, calling my attention back to what's important. Gliding her finger in and out of me with ease, I can't take much more of this, yet here I am, taking it. She climbed back up me, her eyes lit, her skin glowing, her muscles taunt. Why is she so fucking desirable? It's just not fair! Her lips captured mine, silencing me, erupting me. Her, it seems to be her. She tasted strange; I suppose she tastes like me. My heart swelled, my eyes watered, I think I might be fucked. Literally and figuratively.

Her teeth bit into my neck, I then quickly cried out in pain as she tried to add a second finger inside of me. She stopped all movement and sat up. Leaving me cold to the rush of air. Looking at me with a shocked expression. She wiggled her finger inside of me, as if trying to find something. I winced, feeling pained and uncomfortable. Her breathing slowed and shoulders sagged. A perplexed expression on her face.

"You're... You're still a virgin?"

☒

Chapter 9

# Passion & Poetry-Part 3

"You're ...You're still a virgin?" I sniffled as tears burned my eyes. And a second burn, burned me below. Her body stiffened, as she pulled her finger out. I whimpered again, this time in protest. Her beautiful eyes watched me carefully as she seemed to be sorting through her thoughts. Then, like warm sunlight after an unusually long winter, a beautiful smile spread across her lips. "I wasn't wrong about you.... I knew it!" her voice rose with a triumph I didn't quite grasp as she landed on top of me. Her lips feverishly claiming mine. My heart jumped into my throat; she wasn't wrong... About me? Did she believe me? She did! She is the one who used to beat up my exes after they lied about me... It was always her... Does she want to be with me? Like, really?

My thoughts were drowned out by her kissing me. Her body moving with mine. Colliding into me. I never knew that someone could make me feel this, crave this, want this like she does. She has awakened me, and I won't fear it. I will embrace it, arms wide open. I threw my arms around her. My heartbeat rushing in my ears. My chest swelling with disbelief as I kissed her back. I want this, I want her. Even if I'm angry, even though it hurts. It doesn't matter, because for once in my life, I want. And I won't let anything steal this moment from me. With rough, drawn out kisses, she pulled me to the edge of my sanity. Her lips leaving unbearably hot trails down my body. As if she were fire itself. Tasting my skin, savoring my flavor, while setting me ablaze. She leaned above me. Looming over me like an angel of destruction. A deliverer of unquenchable pleasure and insatiable pain. Her sharp eyes held me pressed against the bed. Her red lips parted. Her warm hand resting at the base of my neck with a gentle, yet somewhat alarming squeeze. Her eyes were wild as she watched me. Beautiful, and possibly crazy.

"I am going to take you Stacy. I am going to be the one who claims your body. No one else will take from you what I am going to. No one will have you the same way I am going to have you. No one, because you are mine." Her hand slid down my chest, where she not all too lightly pinched my nipple. I hissed, only to earn a smile of approval. Her hand continued down, as my heart slammed against my chest. She was going agonizingly slow. Her breath warmed my ear. Her voice a saucy liquidation of sexual desire, spoke to me. "I have wanted this for so long Stacy. Wanted you under me. Begging me to do things to you that would make a prostitute blush. I've waited, lost hope many times, and waited still. And now, I have you, you're here."

Again, my eyes widened as her hand cupped my sensitive lower half. Her eyes never leaving mine. Her raw emotion leaving me breathless. Has she spent- oh! My wondering was cut short as her fingers pressed against me. Drawing my attention back to her. I licked my lips, nervously. Trembling under the weight of her steady gaze.

"Tommy I..." my voice hitched in my throat "I think you're my Pandora's box." A small smile curved the edges of her lips. And she leaned in a little closer. "Let me show you what they left out of the storybook then." Her lips collided into mine as her finger pushed into me yet again. I inhaled deeply as she filled me with a single digit. Her eyes not leaving me. With the same amount of passion, she pushed deeper into me. The mixture of the roughness of her finger, and the ease of her glide, made my mind swirl. I closed my eyes, the feelings washing over me. Her finger curved up, rubbing against something that caused me to gasp unexpectedly. And oh so quickly, I was close to the edge again.

"Baby, you are so tight. And so fucking beautiful." she moaned, her finger going faster. I bit my lip, rocking my hips in rhythm of her. "That's it Stacy, show me." I clenched tighter around her, excitement driving my actions. "Oh baby" she whispered, as she moved even faster. Pleasure filled my vision, my core pulsed, my body vibrated. I couldn't breathe as her thumb rubbed against my clit. And an explosion of wetness flowed from me. I tightened around her, trying to hold onto the orgasm that crumbled everything within me. Light kisses dotted my face as she slowly brought me down from my high. My body hummed in the afterglow of pleasure.

Her warm lips brushed my temple as she spoke. "Now that you are relaxed, I want you to take a deep breath, Sweets. Just let me guide you." Wow, she's really good at this. No doubt, she has a lot of experience. Fear tried to build up at the edges of my mind, but I pushed them away and relaxed as she instructed. Keeping still as she continued to move her finger within me. She then bent over me. "Now, I'm going to add the second finger. I want you to stay relaxed, okay babe?" My heart swelled as she supported her body slightly on mine. I closed my eyes. Anticipating the pain. "Shhh, it's okay baby. Just relax. It'll be alright." I took deep breaths. Calming myself down. I've never seen her being so sweet before. It's actually quite amazing.

Then a blinding pain ripped through me. As a secondary burning sensation ached between my legs. I felt like she was stretching me open and forcing more of herself into me. I cried out, tears immediately falling from my eyes. But she didn't stop. Instead, she slowly started pushing deeper into me, growing my blinding pain a little more. The dark room, only lit by the faint light from the hallway, faded from around me. Intense brown eyes watched my every movement as she continued her slow assault. The pain in my core slowly turned into a low burn. In this moment, I'd like to ask myself how I got here. But in truth. I don't care for the answer. Because the object of my misguided obsession had two fingers deep inside of me, and a fire within her eyes. She licked her red lips, her eyes dilated as she pushed deeper still. I clutched the blanket, hissing out in pain. "You're mine now Stacy. You were always mine."

I tried to think of something to say, but nothing came out as she pulled her fingers from me, then back in. I gritted my teeth, trying my best not to cry. But tears burned my vision regardless, spilling over onto my cheeks. I opened my eyes and looked up into hers. Kindness. For the first time, kindness twinkled within her beautiful eyes, shining like stars. "I have always wanted you Stacy. Always dreamt I'd one day have you..." She rested her forehead against mine.

I looked into her eyes. A lightness lifting me off the bed. And without any other words, I pulled her lips against mine. Kissing her like it's our first time. Savoring her, burning her into my memory. She slammed her fingers inside of me, burning pain and shaky pleasure consorted within me. Both fighting for dominance. But pleasure grew as the burning subsided. Her strong body, hot on top of mine. Her scent filling my lungs. I wrapped my arms around her, moaning as she moved within me. "Tommy" I whispered; her muscles flexed under my hands. Her breath rushing past my ear. Overwhelmed by the sheer force of her, I shook as my eyes attempted to roll up into my head. Throbbing and gasping under her, I spread my legs wider. She sat up, hot eyes blazing. "Stacy, fuck..." She moaned. Her fingers pushing faster within me. I can't breathe, she's, she's taking me. I gripped the bed, trying to breathe past the growing pressure in my lower abdomen. Tears continued to fall from my eyes, unintelligible words slurred from my lips. My heart racked against my chest, my entire body tense as her fingers only seemed to increase in speed. Stripping away every ounce of restraint and self-control I've mastered. I cried out, the pressure getting tighter, everything around me but her growing darker. "That's it Stacy, empty out. Cum all over my bed. Release yourself to me."

And then it happened. Lake a taunt rubber band snapping. My body convulsed with the power of my orgasm. Everything stilled for a moment. As bliss like rain showered over me. It ignited my skin, it kissed my clit, it rested within my clenched opening. Blinding, suffocating, invigorating. All words that flashed through my mind as the sweetest glow cooled my heated skin in the wake of what could only be described as earth shattering. Soft kisses decorated my skin, and the wonderful creation that is Tommy J, brushed hair from my eyes. "I have always loved you Stacy

Marie Montro. That is the truth hidden behind all those lies." I wanted to speak, wanted to say something to her. How I've always wanted her affection. How I craved her words even as they hurt me. But everything seemed to disappear, sleep quickly taking me...

Tommy J. Point of view

I watched her, as she laid passed out on my bed. My fingers still trapped within her pulsing folds. I have dreamt of this day. Given up many times, and then it would resurface. Now she lays bare, her nectar soaking into my sheets. Her taste on my tongue. I watched her. Falling in love all over again. Why am I so intrigued and intertwined with her? She will always be my downfall. She will break me. But that is the point of love, isn't it? To love and lose and love again? I looked down; I'll have to clean her up. Blood and womanly cum now stained my sheets. "You and I Stace, we're going to be together for a long while. My siren." I whispered with a smile. My heart pounding loudly in my chest.

I looked up as the door to my room busted open. "Hey Tommy, Imma need you to head out for the night. My girl Dani is coming over..." My dickshit of a brother walked in with flowers and a box of chocolates. Already spewing a lie from his lips. His eyes widened as he took in the scene. He saw a now sleeping Stacy, nude and spread out on my bed with my fingers still inside of her. His face turned white. The items falling from his arms. "What the fuck Tommy!" He yelled looking horrified.

I smirked. Okay, now it's officially the best day ever.

"Shut the fuck up." I said, pulling my fingers from inside of Stace. "D-Did you drug and rape her you Psycho Bitch?" he yelled.

I stood up as he took a threatening step towards me. "Listen here fuck head. Anything we did was 100% consensual. Now if I were you, big bro. I'd be thinking of a way to convince your sister to not tell Daniella, your fiancé, how much of a lying sack of shit you are. Now get the fuck out of my house."

☒

Chapter 10

# Snippet: Kisses

"Would you like a kiss?" Abby asked, her brown eyes bright, her cute smile on the edge of naughty innocence. I was leaned against the wall, outside of class, before the final bell rung.

I smirked, looking down at her adorable self. "Ooookay" I replied slowly, in a low voice. She smiled up at me. Her curly hair bouncing as she jumped in front of me. Unaware of my secondary intentions. Her innocent game, in the hands of a predator, how cute. No point in fighting my nature, she did ask an honest question. I grabbed a hold of her by her waist, confusion in her eyes. I then slammed my lips into hers. A gasp of shock left her as she stood frozen. I pulled her closer, her soft body pressed against mine. Her warmth, heating the chill within. Her lips timidly following my lead. She melted like chocolate on a warm tongue, in my arms. The sound of Hershey kisses hitting the floor echoed around us. It brought a smile to my lips as I kissed her deeper.

With a smirk still on my lips, I pulled back. Her eyes widened, her lips red and trembling. Her cheeks blazing, her breathing rushed. "Thanks, I really needed that." The final bell rung; her shocked eyes turned angry. Her chest puffed up; her fists closed tight.

"Y-you! How dare you!" She's so damn cute. I winked and turned away. Walking into class.

Chapter 11

# Snippet: Shower

Exhausted, I pulled into the driveway. It's been a long day today. My feet hurt from spending overtime in heels, my back feels sore, and I could really use a hot shower and a bottle of old wine... I climbed out of my car with my suitcase in hand. I unlocked my front door and stepped in. Expecting my girl to be on the couch dozing while watching her favorite show. But no, when I walked in, I was greeted by sweetly scented candles lit the otherwise darkened room. Their fragrance calming my stressed mind.

Soft music played, lulling my nerves, and on the side table next to my chair, sat a chilled bottle of wine, a small bowl filled with mini Kit-Kats and Reese's cups, and a note. I picked up the note and read it.

*Dear Kathryn, my sweet and beautiful lover. I wanted to do something special for you, but I might be asleep by the time you get home. I made your favorite for dinner and it's in the oven. Please wake me up if I'm asleep, I want to give you something. I love you* ❤☒ *XOXO Anna.*

I couldn't help the smile that bloomed across my cheeks. She's my joy. It doesn't matter that she's so much younger than me. It doesn't matter that I make most of the money. The fact is, she makes me happy. I've gone far too many years being unhappy with a woman my age and pay grade, who didn't love or appreciate me. I feel happy to come home now, overwhelmingly excited even when exhausted. Smiling to myself, I kicked off my heels and started shedding clothes as I made my way to the bathroom, dropping my dirty clothes into a laundry basket. When the sound of the shower going drew my attention. Yes! She's still awake! Slowly, I eased the bathroom door open, and was greeted by a gust of hot steam and the sweet off-key singing of my lover. I closed the door behind me and watched her through the fogged sliding doors of the shower. She happily sang to the music on her phone while washing her hair. Her cute ass shaking in rhythm with the music. I burn for this girl, ache for her. She's a sexy young thing who doesn't even know how beautiful she is.

Her back was to me, the water causing her soft skin to shine. Without much more thought, I quietly slid the door open and stepped in. She squealed, making a cute noise as I pressed my naked front into her smooth back. "Y-you're home early." I smiled and brushed my lips across her shoulder. A shaky breath escaped her, and my arms circled around her hips, as hot water washed down our naked bodies heating my chilled skin.

"As if work could keep me away from you." I whispered into her ear, causing her to shiver. I licked up her neck with the tip of my tongue. Her skin was clean and soft from a good scrubbing. I want her, I always want her. And I'm going to take her.

I pushed her forward; her hands instantly came up to stop her from hitting the wall. She gasped "Ryan!" I smiled, sliding my leg up between hers. Forcing her to open wider. She is my corruption, my sweetest sin. I know that I can never go back. I have tasted the forbidden, and it's sweet, innocent, energetic, and eager. "Yes baby?"

I lifted my leg up, grazing her slick kitten. It was hot against my knee; her protest trembled and fell from her lips in a discordant stream of unintelligible sounds. "Erring" she moaned as my fingers trailed up her thigh and roughly gripped her beautiful ass. "Yes baby?" I said again enjoying the game. She opened her mouth to speak, and a wicked smile spread across my lips. I slipped my fingers down and in between her wet folds. Snugly resting them at her opening.

My clit jumped in excitement as she pushed herself back against my fingers. Her protest forgotten. Her opening twitched, trying to grasp what's just out of reach. She was breathing heavily now. "Who's my favorite girl?" I circled her increasingly slick opening as she moaned "M-me." I kissed her shoulder. "Who's going to give me her body?" I grazed her clit, causing her to gasp. "I am!" she declared with a desperate plea. "Hmmm, who's going to let me fuck her as much and as hard as I want tonight? Who's going to be my good little girl, and let her Dom possess her?" I gripped her hard clit, she cried out. "I WILL DOMMY!" I smirked "That's such a good girl" and I then plunged my fingers into her.

She hissed deeply, arching her back. With one arm around her, I locked her in place. The other, I pushed my fingers in and out of her hotness. The water was running cool, but I didn't care. No one has made me feel as alive as she has. And come hell or high water, I'm going to please her. "Dommy!" Her moans are the purest. The most mouthwatering, clit pulsing noise I have ever witnessed in my adult life. I crave it, it is my drug, one that even when I have it, I need more! I pulled my fingers from her and turned her around. "What are you-?" I slammed my lips into hers, holding her steady with my body. I need her. I pulled her leg up and around me, hanging it over my hip. Then I pushed my fingers back into her wanting slickness. Her soft chest pushed against mine, her rapid breathing making it rise and fall. She's so beautiful, her brown eyes were dilated. Her wildly curly hair damply stuck to her skin. She was squeezing tight around me. Milking my fingers, her hands gripped my shoulders. "Dommy" she whispered, she's close. I want to see her cum, cum by my hand. And my hand only. "Look at me Anna, I want to see your eyes." Her eyes met mine. Shaking me to the core. The intensity she watched me with knocked the air from my lungs.

Without any more words, we watched each other. I saw the twitch of her shaking lips as her orgasm neared the edge. Her grip tightened. She held her breath. But her eyes never left mine. Heat washed over me; even as cold water fell from the shower head. Her cheeks were flushed, her tongue slipped out and licked the water from her wet lips.

I pushed myself into her faster, harder, she slammed back, forcing herself to keep her eyes open. She moaned louder now, her breathing quickening, then she screamed. Her eyes closed, her head fell back as she begged me to keep going, to not stop, so I didn't. She is the most beautiful sight to my eyes. I love her. "I love you Annalise, my sweet lover." She smiled, her eyes unfocused and glazed over as the heat of her orgasm washed through her. "That’s it baby" I whispered against her ear. My fingers twitching inside of her. "Let me have all of you."

☒

## Chapter 12

# Visit

Clink! I shot up from my bed, hugging my stuffed cow Mr. Moony tightly to my chest. Breathing heavy, I tried to gather my surroundings in the dark. Why am I up? 'Clink!' I looked over at my window as another (what I assume to be a rock) hit it. Getting up I stumbled over and looked down, shocked to see my friend Jen. What the hell? Yawning, I pulled open the window, shivering at the cold chill, and poked my head out. "Why are you waking me up at 3 in the morning Jen?" I quietly yelled down at her.

She ran her hand through her hair, looking up at me. "I'm sorry Meg, but I kinda had a rough night. You gonna let me up?" I looked at her a little longer, then pushed the rope down. Standing back, I 'accidentally' tossed a few items on the floor and crossed my arms. Waiting for her to climb up. I'm on the 2nd floor, so it took a while... With a grunt, she hoisted herself up into my room, trying to catch her breath. "Y-ya know... It would be easier... 'whoo' if you were... 'cough'... on the 1st floor. Why the hell are you up so far?" Shaking my head, I just smiled at her. There are two bedrooms downstairs, but I prefer being higher up. Standing up straight, she looked at me the way she always did. As if trying to see what I was thinking.

"Mind if I crash here tonight?" I looked at her dirty jeans and scruffy sweater. Her black hair doing a wild something on top of her head. Then back into her eyes. "Not in that" I said, walking over to my dresser. "Okay, but I don't want to wear any of those girly night dresses." I raised my eyebrow at her, not that she could see it. "Don't look at me like that woman. You know that those dresses cramp my style" hmm, guess she can.

"Style? Since when do you have style?" I joked. Sticking my tongue out at her. "Ha. Ha. Ha" she laughed sarcastically as I grabbed a large blue T-shirt and tossed it at her. It hit her in the face and she mean mugged me, glaring at me through squinted eyes. I stuck my tongue out at her again. Then decided to play with her, might as well have fun. "You mean this dress?" I said running my hands down my body. I glanced up at her, she was watching me with a very serious look on her face.

Lifting up the sides I did a little dance, letting it raise higher with each sway of my hips. "You know, many would love to see a woman like me in a dress like this." The dress was now up to the top of my thigh, almost showing off the tip of my silk panties. I raised it a fraction higher, giving her the slightest view of them. Glancing up again, her mouth was hanging open. And her eyes as wide as saucers.

Then as fast as I could I ran to my bed with a loud "PSYCH!" Giving her no time to react as I was now buried under my soft lavender blanket. "Damn you woman, you are evil." I again raised my brow at her, she looked away quickly then turned around. "I uh...mean, grow up." I'm sure her face was blood red as she got undressed. The thrill of being ogled by my bestie made my tummy flip and jump in excitement. And a mean, sadistic smile danced on my lips.

Not able to resist as I was already on the edge of doing bad things, I peeked up at her, staring at her strong legs and up. She seemed to glow in the dark, her pale skin picking up any light possible. Black tight sport shorts hugged her waist. Letting it be known that she had a nice firm butt almost begging to be squeezed. She wasn't super muscular but had strength. Her back was curved and sculpted, lightly decorated with a few scars here and there.

She was above all, beautiful. "Fuck!" I jumped up fearing that she had caught me, only to see her bending over holding her foot. "Damn it woman! What the hell is on your floor?" I smiled sheepishly, hiding my pleasure that she stepped on my booby trap. "New pack of dice, I meant to pick them up...sorry." She turned and glared at me, giving me a full view of her breasts. They were even whiter than the rest of her skin and they stood firmly on her chest, like proud orbs of glory. With a soft pink face and pointed nose. Very cute.

"Done raping me with your eyes?" she smirked. Haha, jokes on her. "It's no different than any other times. I've been looking at your body for years" her eyes popped out of her head. "What?" she asked. I laughed. "Oh, come on Jen, I know you're gay. Only a lesbian would come to my house at 3 o'clock in the morning and throw rocks at my window. And then climb two stories to get into my room. You're a lesbian, I know it." I smirked playfully, with every intention of squeezing this for all its worth. Again, she stared at me, with both shock and confusion. "Whaaat?" she asked again, this time slowly, this time afraid. Oh yeah, time to let the real tease out. I noticeably let my eyes travel up and down her mostly nude body. "Nice tits" I said, my voice deep and flowing with seduction. She stood straight, eyeing me with suspicion. "Okay, what the hell happened to you and why?"

I laughed at her. "I'm here, the nicer, censored me disappears when I'm awakened at 3 A.M. So now, you're stuck with this me. Nice ass too" I said, smirking fully. She backed away; the t-shirt still clutched in her hands. "I- I uhh, I think I should get dressed and go... You must be PMS-ing or something." I looked at her, thinking of how to go about this properly... I think I should take off my night gown.

Yeah, that sounds like a wonderful idea. She may not forgive me, but eh who cares. It's 3 in the fucking morning! On a school night! Yeah, I'm gonna make her suffer for it. I was having a wonderful dream too.

I hummed a happy tune and pulled my nightgown from over my head. And dangled it over the edge of the bed. Eyeing her, while biting my lip seductively. Her mouth hung open; her eyes zeroed in on my now exposed upper body. "Ooooh Jeeeeny" her dark eyes slowly rose to my face, causing my skin to warm. I looked her straight in the eyes and let the silky fabric fall to the ground. "Come on baby, let's cuddle." My voice dripped with a thick slice of temptation. I licked my lips slowly, holding her down with my gaze. Oh yeah, she's gonna suffer.

Jen squared her shoulders, cracked her neck, and tossed the blue shirt behind her. And with a voice I can only describe as one of the sexiest voices I've ever heard, she growled at me "Okay, Megan..." and in a deathly, yet beautiful whisper "Let's cuddle." Oh shit. Oh, holy shit! She took three sure footed steps towards my bed, then jumped back screaming "What the fuck!!" She held her foot, yanking something from the bottom. Whoops. She threw it at me, missing me entirely. Looks like she found the jacks I put out for her. That's what she gets for waking me up at 3 o'clock in the morning! I smiled like it was my birthday. Blindly happy that I have gotten my just revenge. But that smile was soon challenged as Jen now glared me down.

"That's it. I'm going to fucking spank you." I laughed at her. "Yeah, right. You think you can? Try me" I hissed. And immediately I regretted it. As she smirked and launched herself over the jacks and on top of me. I squeaked, fighting against her as she pinned my hands above my head. Oh shit. You know that moment, when you realize that the beautiful shaggy bear carpet, is in fact not a carpet? Do you understand that moment? This-this feels like that moment.

Jen glared down at me, her eyes shining with unmistakable anger. "I'm going to spank you now." Having forgotten that she is a swimmer, much to my personal idiocy, she without much effort rolled me onto my stomach. And against my skillful pleading, she held my back down with one incredibly strong hand and spanked my ass with the other. Speaking with every swat. "You. Are. Such. A. Bad. Girl!" I whimpered, finding it odd that I was turned on by this, even though my behind burned. She then turned me over roughly and sat on my stomach. I hissed in pain.

"You, you are... Errr bad! Argh!" She grabbed my wrists and pinned them above my head again, squeezing them tightly. And spoke slowly. "I am going to do what I've wanted to do to you for years. And you, you damn tease. You are going to like it goddammit." She leaned in closer, her strong hands getting tighter. "You're going to not only like it, but you're going to beg for more." I looked up at her, unable to hide my smirk, though I am curious. She's a virgin, I know it. So, this is all a big, well played bluff.

"Oh really? You seem pretty confident, but you have no resume to back that up." She leaned in closer, her face no more than a few inches from mine. I could feel the heat of her body, the hotness of her core pressed against my stomach. Turning me on bad as pain tangled with pleasure, fogging up everything else but her. Her tight black shorts did nothing to withhold her heat, if anything it made it spread evenly across my stomach. Despite my distraction, I noticed that I didn't get the 'yeah, you're right' I was expecting. No, what I got was a verbal swift kick in the chest as she started laughing.

"Megan, Megan, Megan. You poor innocent thing. You ever wonder why Sarah Dolins always has sleepovers? At least twice a month?" I frowned. "No, Sarah only has them once every few months." She smirked, "Not with me." My mouth dropped open in disbelief. This can't be real. Anyways that's only one person. "Doesn't matter" I said with my chin held high. "Even if, and trust me, I'm really stressing the IF. If that's true, you've only been with one person. All women are not the same." I smiled triumphantly. Again, she shook her head and laughed. "Who ever said it was just Sarah and I at our private sessions?"

"Fuck" shit. I'm gonna kill Sarah. I'm not jealous... Just offended that I was never invited. Jen smiled. "Fuck is correct. Now that my references check out; Let's see if I can make you nervous." Oh no, this is revenge. Revenge for all those years I've teased and tested her. Full well knowing that she was gay. Shit, why am I so turned on by this? Her hands tightened on my wrists, making them hurt. Why does it feel good? She crashed her lips into mine, taking my air away. Her lips were soft and firm as they moved against mine. It was the hottest sensation I have ever felt. Her lips bruised me blissfully, and she started grinding her core into my stomach. "Wow" I mumbled against her lips. I could feel the dampness of her shorts and struggled to keep my cool. My best friend is dry humping me... Damn this is good.

I looked up at her, a deep hunger growing in me. I want to be in control. I fought for control, determined that I'll be on top of this. I pulled with all my strength to free my wrists and bucked my hips. But in response she only gripped my wrists tighter and rocked her hips harder. Weakening my resolve and reducing me to soft moans and helpless whimpers. When she had me calm, she bit my lip and smoothly eased her tongue in. My core leaped in excitement, my legs squeezed together, trying to keep the heat from pouring out of me. How is she doing this? A breathless moan slipped out as she nibbled my bottom lip.

"You are mine" she growled into my ear, causing my whole body to shake in lust. Fuck, I've never been this turned on before. God she's so hot. I could feel the wetness slowly leaking out of my opening, my panties completely damp. Her soft tongue flicked against my earlobe as she continued speaking. "I'm going to let go of your wrists now. And if you move them, you will regret it. Am I understood?" I nodded quickly, not able to trust my voice. "Mmmm, that's a good girl, a very good girl."

One hand released my wrists and traced lightly down my arm to my shoulder, igniting sparks along my flesh. Her lips trailed down, kissing me lightly till she reached my neck. Biting into it, a loud gasp jumped from my chest.

I didn't notice what her hand was doing as she sucked a sweet spot on my neck that had me seeing rainbows. I didn't notice it till it cupped one of my breasts proudly and with all the confidence in the world. Her warm hand caressed it lovingly, my heart slammed against my chest as I looked up at her... My best friend, the girl I've always loved, looked back at me. I licked my lips, trying to slow my breathing. She simply smiled down at me, loving it. Her eyes held a fire, her voice kissed by angels. I felt vulnerable and entrapped in her gaze. Her eyes shined, her lips red and puffed from our kissing.

Then a tingling sensation shot through me as her fingertips grazed over my hardened nipple. My eyes widened; a shaky moan broke out of my open lips. She smiled down at me and did it again. Getting the same response. "Always so beautiful Meg, So... Sensual." Her tongue ran across her lips as she captured my nipple between her fingers and gently rolled it back and forth. My clit pulsed, begging for relief. And she watched me. Watched every emotion in my face, listened to every moan and whimper. She fed off of it. Sliding down my body, she sent light kisses down my shoulder. "J-Jen? Wh-what are yoooooooou" my mind scrambled as her tongue circled the tip of my nipple and her hot mouth enclosed around it. My hips jerked up as a silent scream left my lips. I was hot, I felt like my body was on fire under her touch. She nibbled the tip of my bud and pinched the other. Sending shock waves of pleasure through me. My core pulsed so powerfully it almost hurt, and my moans grew louder, my shaking continued. I wanted to grab her, pull her closer to me. But I didn't move, her eyes held me down with a silent threat.

Her tongue was heaven, so soft and warm as her teeth held my nip in place. Flicking back and forth with her flexible appendage. "Please" I moaned. Not sure what I'm asking for, but knowing I need it. I need her. I've always needed her. I'll always need her. "Please what?" she asked, her tongue tracing little patterns on my breast, occasionally running over the raised tip. Each time causing me to whimper in ecstasy. "Jen, please" I begged again, this time with more desperation. She sat up, looking down at me and growled softly, "You know what I want to hear Megan. Please what?" I whimpered, at her mercy. "Please take me." She growled; a primal kind of growl I've only heard animals make. Her hand came down and cupped my soaked kitten, we both moaned in unison. "Damn Meg, you're hot..." Her finger pressed into my thin underwear, gently going up and down my slit. "And wet... For me." Her dark eyes locked with mine. I whimpered, my legs rubbing together as she teased the outside of my panties.

"Please" rocking my hips I tried to create friction. But her touch remained light, ghostly even. "Mmmm, I like the sound of you begging." She removed my underwear, making a slow torturous tease of raking her nails gently down my legs, and grasping my thighs. She occasionally brushed her thumb against my clit, enjoying my cries for mercy. Yet even so, she continued her light touch up and down my slit. "Beg some more." I stuck my chin out instantly defensive. "No" I said, putting on a big front. I can resist her. "No?" she asked, her voice heavy and thick with lust. Fuck that's sexy, she's still very much in control. "N-no" I said again, less confident. One of her long, strong fingers slipped into my folds gliding across my clit. Holy mercy!

"Beg!" she barked touching it harder. I moaned deeply, closing my eyes. She's going to break me. "Please" I whispered. "What?" she asked, knowing exactly what I said. "Please Fuck me!" I yelled. Not concerned about my brother or parents. She slammed a single finger into me, causing stars to float around the room. But she didn't move it, instead, she crawled up, and took a fistful of my hair. "Mine" she growled, pulling her finger all the way out. And with force, she slammed it all the way in me again. "Mine" and again. "Mine" and again. My core blissfully ignited on fire, clenching and relaxing with the force of Jen's movements.

I was moaning under her, my legs spread, my head spinning and my heart raging. And I'm not even sure if I'm breathing. How can one, one single finger make it feel this good?!?! This... This is too good. This is wonderful, magical. Is this what I've been missing?! I screamed on the inside as she pulled my hair and added a second finger. Stretching me open and speaking into my ear. "You're so tight baby, so sexy, you fucking goddess. And you're mine." She pushed the two deeper into me, curving them up. I can't breathe, my fists were closed tightly, needing something to help displace the growing pressure inside of me.

"I am going to fuck you over and over. Tonight, tomorrow, and from this day forward." My core clenched impossibly tighter around her fingers, what the hell is she doing to me!?! "We're staying home sick tomorrow, and I'm going to do so many pleasurable things to you."

Her fingers moved faster in and out of me. Despite my hold on them. "You're gushing baby, cum for me" she whispered and bit hard into my neck. My eyes closed as she went even faster. Pulling my hair and biting my neck, white light seemed to burn into me. A ball of fire erupted in me, braking out in waves of uncensored pleasure.

Her free hand clamped over my mouth as I loudly moaned out with the force of my flooding release. The whole while she continued to push into me, whispering all the wonderful things she plans on doing to and with me. "My sexy, beautiful girl" she whispered as her fingers slowed down to a gentle caressing. "This is only the beginning."

⊠

Chapter 13

# Snippet: Jump

Come on!" "Whoo! Do it!" "Don't be afraid, jump!" I stood at the edge of a cliff, the sun falling into the distance, igniting the horizon. My friends are down below, in the water. Encouraging me to take a not so blind leap. I took a deep breath. Terrified, my heart was racing. My hands felt clammy, my stomach urpy. I think I'm going to be sick. I - I can't do this! I shook my head and turned around. Ready to go back to the car in defeat when someone stopped me. She's new to our group. Doesn't talk much. Honestly, this is the first time we've hung out. Which only added to my shame. My other friends already know I'm a coward, now she does too. I looked away. "Hey" she said, her hand reaching out to take mine. "Yeah?" I glanced up at her. She had dark hair, dark eyes, and light skin. She speaks with an accent because she's from the Ukraine or something like that. Her name is Ta'lona. "Do not be frightened friend." I smiled sadly at her. She doesn't understand how wimpy I am. "I will show you, sometimes living on the edge can be... how you say... um... thrilling?"

With my hand in hers, she led me back to the edge, I was intrigued on how she'd handle this. All of my friends have tried. I'm incurable. She stood behind me. "Don't push me." I warned, already feeling nauseous. "I would not, my friend." She turned me around to face her. "The thrill of jumping is the power of not knowing. Everything in your life is predictable. But when you take matters into your hands, then you own the joy of the unpredictable." She stepped closer to me. "If you jump, you know you will hit the water, you know it may hurt. If you land wrong, you could stop your heart or pass out. You may bust a lung and not be able to breathe... If you walk away, you'll go back to your car, hear us laughing from the safety of your locked door. You'll go home and tell your mama or papa that you had fun though it would be a lie. They will ask you to do this again and you'll say yes thinking that next time...next time...no, next time you'll have the courage. And when you're old and gray, because I assure you, you'll live that long... You'll ask yourself if next time ever came. You'll ask if you ever really tasted the edge and experienced the thrill. You know what the answer will be. However, I leave you with a choice. Go back to your car, where it is safe. Or stand with me, and do something wild, something dangerous, something reckless. And take that leap. Take this jump. And if you have to close your eyes to do it. Then do it. Because I will be here. Just as reckless and stupid as you."

I stared at her in shock. She should be a political speaker or something. She's got it down. I glanced over my shoulder. Looking down. But she grabbed my chin. "Don't look down, my girl. Look at me." Shaking, I nodded my head. I know she's right. I've been doing it for years already. Telling myself that someday I'll be braver. Now or never. "Okay Talo" I whispered, still very much afraid. She smiled at me. "Good, now here is something that will help with the unexpectedness of your fall." And with that, her lips smacked into mine. Shocking my system and stealing my air. I should have known that when she kissed me, I'd jump back in shock. But I didn't. I felt myself falling fast down to the water. I hit feet first into the cold lake that engulfed me and pulled me under with a splash. My heart was screaming, my blood boiling as I surfaced. A splash hit me in the face, the waves of it rocking me away. I glared at her as she surfaced. My friends were cheering, pleased and stunned that she was able to make me take the leap.

"You pushed me!" I yelled at her, which caused my friends to instantly quiet. She turned and looked at me, her cheeks a soft blush of pink with the thrill of jumping. "I did not" she replied calmly; I swam closer to her. "Yes, you did! You kissed me and-"

She nodded. "And you jumped back, I had no control over your actions my friend. And for once, neither did you. So, though your argument has a substantial base, it is not valid." I pouted. Angry. "Well...you tricked me and kissed me."

"Yes, indeed I did. Yet I would have done almost anything to be gifted the opportunity to taste your lips, my friend." I stared at her with my mouth hanging open. "What are you a lawyer?" She shook her head with a blinding grin. "I am not."

☒

Chapter 14

# Snippet: Say What Now

Come on babe" she shook her head back and forth. Making her braids resettle. "No Rye, there is no way we are doing that here. No way in hell."

"But-"

"Hell itself will freeze over. And I'm not just talking about the first layer. All seven, plus Gehenna, and all of Tartarus..." I looked blankly at her. "Wha-"

"And the Abyss. All six hundred and sixty-six levels will freeze solid before I let you, finger me, in the bathroom, of an airplane." Damn... Guess I'm going to have to try harder.

☒

Chapter 15

# Something Old

I looked in the mirror. Taking slow deep breaths. Today is the day. One of the most important days of my life. It starts here. My dress flowed to the ground like silky white rivers. My hair braided up into a bun. Diamond earrings shining like tear drops against my cheek. Today is the last day to be unsure.

I should be the blushing bride. Filled with unimaginable amounts of joy, but I'm not. How can I be without her here? She was my rock for so long. Yet she'll let me walk alone... I wiped the single tear that escaped and took one last look at myself, only getting depressed. I'm not-

"Beautiful" I turned around with wide eyes. "KELLY!" I screamed and ran into to her arms. I knew she wouldn't ditch me! Only in her arms have I felt the safest. Burying my head into her neck I inhaled her rustic, slightly masculine scent. Her warmth wrapped around me.

"Didn't think I've forgotten, did you?" she said with a chuckle. I pulled back and looked into her eyes. Remembering when Tom and I announced our wedding and her storming off. That was eight months ago. Eight months without her here to help me and keep me sound.

"Then why did you leave? " I asked. She looked conflicted, biting her full lower lip.

"I had to grow up Sash, couldn't do that with you around." The fuck?

"What the hell do you mean 'couldn't grow up with me around'? You inconsiderate ass!" I pushed away from her. Angry. Who the hell does she think she is? She left so she could do what? She's always been the adult while growing up, so what's the deal now?

Again, she only stood there biting her damn lip. "Answer me before I rip you a new one." Her eyes sparked with something, something I've only seen a few times before with her. Tears.

"Kelly?"

"You know I tried..." she whispered looking down. "Tried to leave you alone, so you could get married and be happy. Maybe have a few kids along the way. Live a life that normal women live... But I can't, the thought of you with anyone makes me damn near crazy." What? "I... I get scared, thinking of him touching you" she paused. "Or kissing you, because no matter how far I run or what I do to keep busy, I can't escape the fact that I love you and if anyone should be kissing and loving you, it should be me."

I was shocked, lost for words. With wide eyes and my mouth hanging open, I was stuck. I mean, I know she loves me... But, not like that... That's... Wrong? Isn't it?

"I know I'm selfish, and I should have said it sooner. I'm sorry. A-and if nothing more, if you do go get married to him, let me at least give you my present." Is it wrong? I've always heard that it was...

Only a few stutter 'I's left my lips in response. She nodded and slowly reached into her pocket, then pulled out a small gold chain. It had a single rose gold heart dangling from it. Instantly, I recognized it. I gave it to her when we were barely old enough to tie our shoes. "I never lost it, because it was more than just a bracelet. It was your heart." With that, she gently grabbed my hand and clipped it onto my wrist. "Something Old, right?"

I nodded, feeling the burning of tears in my eyes. "And something new" she said. In a split second, she had my face in her hands. And her lips on mine. I was entrapped, shock spread throughout my whole body as the fear of my hidden desires bloomed within me. The softness of her kiss and the love that poured out of her had my heart racing to the heavens. The naughty desire grew inside of me. This must be what Eve felt when she tasted the forbidden fruit.

I opened my eyes to see Kelly's steady grays looking intently into me. Her tongue sliding into my mouth. I melted into her, letting go of everything and only seeing her, for a moment at least. As if for the first time, I was home. My hands snaked around her, holding her close. Scared that she may disappear into smoke if I don't hold her tight enough. But she slowly pulled herself away. Ending the best kiss I've ever experienced. Fresh tears were running down her cheeks. New fear filling me. "I will always love you Sasha Lovier Ebony Winslow, no matter what." She gently kissed my cheek. And as fast as she came...she left.

Almost immediately my mom walked in. Giving me no time to process my emotions. She never really liked Kelly; her liking women had everything to do with it. My parents are very much against gay people. She looked behind her then at me." What did she say to you?" I shook my head, "N-nothing Mom" she glared at me. "I don't like that one. I just don't understand why you keep her around. She's bad news. And frankly, I'd rather her not be anywhere near you." I just looked blankly at the ground. Fighting off tears and fears. "Mom please, not now."

She stepped up and tucked a ringlet of hair behind my ear. "Whatever the problem is, it doesn't matter. Today is your day baby girl. You're a bride, and Tom is waiting for you. Just one more hour and you'll be in the most important union of your life" I nodded, holding in my growing fears. "Mom, c-can you stall for a while please? I need a few hours to put myself together." She agreed and patted my hand. "It's okay, everyone gets cold feet dear. I'll come back in two hours for you. I know you'll be ready; you love Tom. He's a good man who loves you." She left, closing the door quietly behind her.

I leaned against the wall, my mind blank. Time seemed to go by as I tried sorting through all that just happened. My best friend not only just confessed HER love for me... She also gave me a mind-blowing kiss and an impossible choice. My eyes fell down to the chain around my wrist. She kept it. I didn't... I forgot about that. She was always the cool one. The hot one who had it together. Does she know my private thoughts when I'm alone? My secret and forbidden desires? My lips tingled; my chest ached. If I could, I'd choose her. I love her, and I'd throw caution to the wind. But I can't, I can never let that darkness leave me. And what about Tom? He really is a good guy. He'll make a good father; he'll be great with the kids. He's kind and caring. A good... husband. Even now, it sent minor chills through me. I may not be in love with him, but I... I can grow to love him, I know it. I want children someday; I want my parent's love and support.

But Kelly... I do love her; I've always loved her. But she's a, a she... I never even really thought of her in that way... At least not when anyone was around. But for years I watched her. Gazing at her while my stomach dropped to the floor. Letting visions of her and other women flow through me when I was with Tom. I know what I am, I know what I have to be, and I know what I can't be.

I slid to the ground. What do I do? I know I have to go out there and marry Tom... I can't run away with her. No one can ever know that this happened. She just unloaded a shit ton of information and emotions on me. What if she tells, would she do that? No, no she can't, I'm not strong like her, I won't ever be strong in that way. But what if she leaves and doesn't come back? Would it be a bad thing then? God will turn his back on me, I've been fighting my whole life to stay good. But the fear of losing her weighed on me. What if I can't find her? What if she realizes that I want her that way? What if I'm making a mistake? What if I'm not though? I don't know how to feel!

Kelly... Kelly... I love her. I can't let her leave me. I know I can never be with her. But I can't let her go. I need her. I'm torn. Because I know that even in my confusion and fears, one thing is certain I cannot be gay. I can't love her in that way, no matter how much I do. And though it makes my heart clench, I refuse to. It's against my own code. She can be whatever she wants, and she is, she is what she is, so boldly, but I can't be. I'd lose my family, all my friends, I won't be able to have kids... But

I'd have her. I just, I don't think I can jeopardize everything for something I know I could never be. She'll leave me for good now... She'll never forgive me...

My lips still tingled, the bracelet glittering in the light. My heart. My heart breaking. Fuck! I... I know I have to let her go. But I don't know if I can. The pain that filled me now was far worse than before. Because now I know the truth, that she loves me. That she's in love with me. I feel helpless and weak. Empty knowing that I can never return it. Kelly. I can't, I can't let her disappear again! I pushed myself up and hiked up my dress. Running out of the room, and down the hall. Ignoring guests and pushing past my Mother calling after me. Only thinking of Kelly. My hair fell out of its bun, bursting into wild ringlets down my back. I slammed through the church doors and ran to the street.

Gasping for air and crying, I looked back and forth, hoping to see her motorcycle. But it wasn't there, she was gone... Gone. I fell to the ground in tears. Did she wait, does she hate me? My heart slamming in my chest. She was my best friend; my true happiness was with her. And that too, was now gone. I dropped my head into my hands, crying my heart out. My chest twisted at the realization that I may never see her again...

My Mom soon found me, laying on the pavement. A complete mess. And all I could manage to say, was that Kelly left me. She gave me a small amount of sympathy, then reminded me of my duty. That my husband is waiting at the alter for me. On shaking legs and a broken heart I stood up. Kelly's gone. I need to let her go. Even if I don't want to. Because this is who I am, this is who I have to be. Nothing else matters. I must get ready. I'm getting married.

☒

Chapter 16

# Something New-Part 1

Kelly's Point of view I had waited for her. Sat outside the church doors for over an hour... Praying to a God I didn't know, that she would come out and love me. I set all my cards on the table. I emptied my heart and exposed myself. But she didn't, she didn't come. She never called. Not a single word, not a single text. So, I stayed gone... It was as if she killed me. If I meant so little to the woman who captured my heart. But days turned to weeks, weeks to months, and months to years. Yet I never received a single thing from her. Not on my phone. Not on Facebook. I questioned whether I was even alive to her. Because I felt dead. As if she had buried me that night. Buried me alive, with no warning. Not even a goodbye.

But I saw her, saw what she's been up to. I respect Tom. He's a good man, and trust there are few left. My anger isn't from her marrying him. I told her the truth, that I would always love her. However, I guess I didn't take the fact that she would completely let me go into consideration. So, after a few years I started learning to let her go. I got some therapy, I moved away. Everything I needed to do, to start over. I even continued my old passion.

I loved photography, and after getting back into the swing of it, I was offered a job by a modeling agency. It was fucking exciting. Stationed in 26 states, Brazil, France, Canada, and Puerto Rico. I've traveled, experienced the natural beauty of the world, and more is yet to be discovered. I have moved on. I must admit though, it's easy to be a player. I get loads of... young stars wanting a leg up, so to speak. Though that's not how I get my lay. It does impress them that I'm so grounded before age 30.

I shrugged my shoulders and looked down at the cutie below me. Wild red hair and beautiful baby blues looked up at me. I met her at the gym some time ago, she's pretty, sexy, and sweet. Always carrying a blinding smile, with a hint of naughtiness, and an innocent nature. I'm not looking for a relationship, but I can't deny that this one is fun to be around. Joyful, funny, and sometimes very gullible. With an amazingly fast mind and untainted talent. Antha's beautiful big eyes looked up at me in a mixture of admiration, lust, and fear. She's a young one, barely 18, college kid. I smirked down at her, leaning in close. "So beautiful, are you sure you want to take a ride? "Her bottom lip quivered, but she nodded her head still.

I brushed my lips softly over her ear. Talking in a deep sensual voice, "I don't go easy kitten..." I gently bit her ear. "I like it rough." Her breathing increased as I brushed my hand down her body. Softly touching her smooth candy trail. Teasing the elastic of her gym shorts. We've been hanging out for a few weeks while I've been off work. Do to my interesting job, I usually work without a vacation for an extended period of time. However, it allows me to have long vacations, so I've had time to cultivate our friendship.

"I I-I'm rrready" her sweet voice fighting so hard to stay under control. She's not only a baby lesbian, but is currently holding tight onto her V card, which I will gladly confiscate. Somewhat shocking to me, I really do seem to like this girl. She makes me happy. Honestly, it's a hard thing to find these days. Someone that you get excited about when you know you're going to see them. Shit, I don't think that's a good sign.

Moving my brain on to more important matters, I looked over her beautiful body. Again, those clear eyes watched me. She has a knack for intensity, and it brought a smile to my lips. Slowly, I hooked my thumbs under her shorts, and eased them off her, underwear included. She could protest, but she didn't. Silently watching me, with pink cheeks and nervously biting her bottom lip. Unknowingly turning me on. I looked down at her mons with a grin. She's a natural red alright. A nice clean triangle connected to her candy trail, pointed down to her slit. Guiding my way to her treasure.

She rushed her hands down to cover herself, but I stopped her. "Don't. You're beautiful Sweets." She looked up at me, a shine of tears in her eyes. I know she's nervous, and scared. Hell, everyone is during their first time. I sure as hell was. Her eyes shined with curiosity, with admiration, with misguided affection. I never understood how it was so easy to make them fall for me. Yet the one I truly wanted...didn't.

I gently brushed her hair out of her face. And kissed her sweet lips. All the while, my hand made quick work of trailing up and down her damp slit. I eased my fingertips between her hot folds, biting back a moan as my clit throbbed. With the flick of my finger, I tickled her pearl, it was already hard and blazing hot under my touch. Mmm, I want to taste her.

I pressed my lips against hers, as my fingers played with her slick bud. She moaned, her lips vibrating against mine. I then led kisses down her jaw, to her neck, and sucked on her sweet spot; every woman has one; eliciting another moan from her. Ahh, music to my ears. She pushed her hips up against my fingers, almost in a silent plea, asking for more. Such a good girl, asking nicely. I smirked to myself, my lips pressed against her throat as I began circling her damp opening. Her muscles tried to clench around my finger, just barely out of reach. I'm getting turned on by her breathless moans and her beautiful body grinding under mine. I lifted myself up and looked down at her. "Are you ready?" I asked.

She quickly nodded her head and bit her bottom lip. She's nervous, I'll go easy on the cutie. I repositioned myself above her. Her wild hair spread elegantly across her pillow. Her cheeks flushed, her chest raising and falling. Mmm, I slid my fingers down her slit, then back up, coating them in her slick wetness. Her clit jumped under the graze of my nails. She hissed, her hips rising off the bed. I smiled at her, she's expressive. I'd love to taste her nectar, but I don't know if I can hold out much longer. I licked my lips, her eyes closed as I began rubbing her with a bit more aggression. Her breath caught in her throat as she gasped under my hand. Rubbing her harder, her hips rocking wildly. I bit my lip as I watched her. She really is a beauty. She was moaning louder, her nails digging into my shoulder. She's close. Her body began to shake.

Hot wetness poured out of her, it was slick and there was plenty of it. "Mmm, baby you made a mess." Taking my hand from her slit, I brought them to her full pink lips. "Taste" I commanded. She eagerly opened her mouth to take in her wetness. She made a face at the taste but continued to lap up her sweet juices. "Good girl" I moaned. Her tongue was running up and down my fingers just right. Talking my hand from her mouth I put it back under her... Then stopped. I want to taste her now. I have to leave this weekend, back to Brazil for a summer photo shoot job. Who knows when I'll be back.

I sat up, between her legs. Taking a look at this beautiful woman. Her eyes stared into me, causing a shiver to run through my body. Damn, she really is something. "Spread 'em wide, little girl" a blush bloomed over her cheeks as she widened her already open legs, giving me a wonderful view. I leaned over her, pushing her legs even further apart and neared her sweet Iris. It was pink, copper red hair, shining and damp from our play. Her lips open, revealing a hidden place for the bold at heart. Her scent erupted around me, more potent the closer I grew, until I was right there. A tongues width away. Her legs shaking and her hips still on their slow rock. The anticipation grinding on her fragile nerves.

I took a deep breath. Blowing cool air onto her exposed clit. She jumped, squeaking. Hahaha, cute. And without further ado, I kissed her delicate lips. Easing my tongue into her tasteful folds. Her hair was soft, and it tickled my nose. She was slick, and her womanly musk filled my surroundings. Sliding my tongue up, I pressed hard against her clit, it was rock solid and smooth. Pulsing lightly under my touch, and demanding attention. My core throbbed at her taste, her smell, and the feel of her.

Her hips slammed against my face. Her movements becoming sporadic and wild as she neared her high. I locked my arms around her thighs, keeping her still. She sang a chorus of whimpers and moans, soft pleas, and incoherent words of bliss. How'd she know that's my favorite song? With an inside chuckle, I attacked her clit, nipping and licking at its smooth surface. Switching from gentle to rough randomly, driving her beyond insane. Her ragged cries filled the room, as she pulled my hair, begging me not to stop!

But I did. I stopped just as she was on the edge of her orgasm. Stopped just as she was about to climb higher and higher towards her desired destination. She whimpered in protest. Her body falling limp. "Oh no, I'm not done with you yet Antha. Far from it." I said with a devilish smile.

Her eyes were dilated and clouded with lust. Her lips were red and swollen. I bet she's a biter. Damn, why do I have to leave so soon? Maybe I'll run into her when I get back... Maybe she'll already be taken. No, I won't think about that now, I only want to feel. Her eyes locked with mine, a kind smile touched my lips, and a saucy one bloomed across hers. The moment she paused in her ragged breathing, was the moment I pushed two fingers into her.

Her tight walls resisted as I invaded her intimate space. The scream that left her could have been heard around the world. Her eyes squeezed shut as she held tightly onto me. I didn't move my fingers. Just resting them inside of her until the pain eased. After several deep breaths, her watery eyes opened, and looked right into me. Damn. She could make a nun swoon with those eyes.

Ever so slowly I moved my fingers in and out. With long drawn out strokes. Eventually, her hips began to rock with me. Her red lips parting as a guttural moan escaped her. I curved my fingers up, rubbing heavily on the wonderful swell of her G spot. "Mmm Kelly, I... It feels so good" Ahh, sounds like music. I know I'm damp. I know I'm turned on. I know I could have this beautiful flower eat me out. But first...

I sat up, and pushed her leg up, using my free hand. As I began to pump with a vengeance. She silently screamed out. Her face contorting into a unique mixture discomfort and ecstasy. Her hands fisted the bed, tears slid down her red cheeks. Yet her hips only increased in speed, riding my fingers stroke for stroke. Squeezing and pulling me in.

Fuck! I watched her, I'm so turned on, I want to take her all over again. I'm not done yet though. The pain left her face as her speed increased. I released her leg and fell on top of her. Rocking my hips into her. Pushing even faster. Her hips bucked up; her arms clung to me. "Kelly! Oh god Kelly!!" She cried out as she began to shake. "Bite me" I moaned into her ear. Without a second of pause, her teeth bit hard into my shoulder. "FUCK!" I groaned, breathing heavy. Her virgin walls encased my fingers in a vice like grip. Pumping me, as hot fluids sprung from around the tight space of her filled opening. Her insides pulsed, her heart raging. Her teeth still embedded in my skin.

My clit ached with each pulse of her walls around my fingers. As a calmness settled over me. A wiping away of the stress and overwhelming emotions. A primal need temporarily quenched. An itch scratched. I twitched my fingers slightly inside of her. Causing her to hiss each time. With my thumb, I touched her clit. It was soft and wet, perfect. Gently, I pulled my fingers out of her and looked at my handy work.

Soft moans left her as her eyes grew heavy. A fresh sheen of sweat cooled on her skin. Her beauty blinding to that of lesser people. Using part of the bed sheet, I cleaned her off. Smart girl, using red sheets. I bent over and gently kissed her soft lips. "Mmm... mmm" She moaned again as sleep took her from me. I left a note on her pillow. And one more kiss for the road. I know she'll be taken by the time I come back. I just hope her next woman treats her right. She deserves that. With one last look, as if trying to capture the image in my memory, I turned to leave. Feeling oddly sadder than I should.

⊠

Chapter 17

# Something New-Part 2

I stood in my empty apartment as movers unloaded boxes from a U-Haul. Wow, I can't believe it's been so long since I've been back. Job after job kept me away. But my bank account is bulging with joy, and now I have some time off. Though I can't complain about my job. I am honored to work with the Merrick modeling agency. And it's not like anything is keeping me tied here. Again, I looked around, beautiful hardwood floors, big open windows, it's a perfect loft. I walked over to one of the windows, looking down. People busied themselves like ants on the sidewalks. Cars passed by and the general activity of the city continued on. Well damn, I'm really missing the wildness of the Brazilian rainforest. I just can't win...

I sat on the edge of the window seat. Still watching as the movers filled my apartment... When my eyes drifted down the street to the gym. Huh, it's not like I'm needing a workout, but it wouldn't hurt to stay in shape. The last thing I want is to lose muscle mass.

Once the movers were finished, I tipped them then searched for my gym bag. An hour later, I was packed and ready to go. I locked up my apartment and headed down the street. I weaved through the lines of people with ease, while avoiding being tripped or crashing into stationary objects. I Crossed the congested street, as my mind asked me if I should consider moving to a more secluded area. Deciding not to think about it just yet, I walked in. Women and a few guys dotted the busy gym. I walked over to renew my membership, then began killing my body....

After a gruesome workout, I headed to the locker room for a quick rinse. The water sprayed over my body, cooling my skin, washing away the sweat and grime of the two-hour workout. Voices could be heard throughout the girl's bathroom. When one tickled my memory. "No, I just... I just don't like him."

"But he was so hot!"

"Not to me..."

"What's wrong with you? He was totally checking you out! You have to at least try. What the heck are you waiting for?"

I turned off the shower and dried off. Pulling a clean sports bra and gym shorts on. I walked around to the lockers where they stood, and a cute redhead caught my eyes immediately. Antha. I stepped forward, her eyes locking with mine. Her friend's back was turned as she waited for Antha to continue. I smiled at her, her beautiful eyes sparkling. She ran past her friend and jumped into my arms. I was a bit stunned but caught her nonetheless, holding her tightly. She smelled of strawberries and lemon. Her curly hair tickling my cheek.

"Kelly, I... I didn't think I'd see you again!" She hugged me tighter. The warmth of her hug, grounding me. She's such a sweet kid. She released me, a blush blooming across her adorable, freckled cheeks. I smirked down at her, completely forgetting about her friend. "Antha, how have you been?" She blushed deeper, looking down. "I'm good Kelly... Um, how are you?" I took her hand, her eyes lifting up to meet mine. "I'm far better now," It was like fire standing so close to her again. I want her, and she's still responding to me, as if no time has passed. "Can I take you to dinner sometime?" She blushed, but nodded quickly, giving me her number. Her friend watched confused as I kissed Antha's cheek and walked out. Well, I'm sure she has some explaining to do...

I didn't seduce her on our first date, though I wanted to. I didn't because a part of me really wanted to have a relationship with her. I took her to dinner, then a walk in the park. Our next date, I took her to an animal rescue facility, and we helped feed baby wild birds. She loves animals. She is going to be an animal rescue and science researcher of disease and prevention. Whatever the hell that is. But she loves doing it. Days turned to weeks of us seeking each other. Every encounter more pleasant than the last. Until one evening, I dropped her off at her dorm. She fiddled with her keys, looking down. Her cheeks pink, her eyes conflicted. "Antha?"

"Wouldyouliketocomein?!" She blurted in a nervous run-on sentence. I grinned and stepped closer to her. "Yes, I would" she blushed deeper and opened the door. Still hiding behind her shy smile. She still wants me. How about that?

The look of the room completely faded away when the door closed behind me. The only thing that existed was her and I. Resting my hands on her hips, I turned her around. Tilted her chin up and brushed my lips against hers. The excitement I felt as her arms circled around my neck was somewhat unnerving. Her movements were unsure. Not yet matured in confidence at her age.

Our lips played the game, hers were soft allowing me to take the lead, I teased her sweet tongue. I disengaged myself from her temporarily, pushing her backwards as I advanced. I then lowered myself onto her couch. She stood there, watching me. "Hey babe, wane sit in my lap?" I asked playfully. She bit her bottom lip and slowly eased herself onto my lap, straddling me. Mum, I could already feel the heat of her core as she adjusted herself. I grabbed her hips and yanked her forward. She gasped, clinging onto my shirt tightly. "You are so sexy Antha. Why are you still single?" I asked. My thumbs tracing little circles on her skin. She glanced away. Thinking about her response. "I... I donor. I guess... I'm just waiting for the right one." Her eyes flickered to me, then away quickly. I squinted my eyes at her. Then a smile broke free.

Well then, let's enjoy each other until the right one arrives." She smiled and nodded her head. I don't want to think that she might think I'm the one. At any given moment my job could pull me away again. I tilted her chin down and brushed my lips across hers. Her sweetness filling me whole. I think I'm going to actually miss her when I leave again. Dread loomed over me, but I pushed it away. I continued to capture her lips with mine. My hands on her waist, I began rocking her hips slowly black and forth, causing her to moan. Damn, she's so responsive.

I nuzzled her neck, her pulse racing under my lips. mom, visions of her begging under me filled my mind. That's it, I must have her. I nipped the soft flesh of her skin, she hissed from the small amount of pain. With my hands secured on her hips, I rocked her a little rougher. Drawing out a deeper moan from her. Her arms latched onto me as her core heated my upper thighs. Fuck she's hot, her curly hair bouncing, her cheeks pink, her lips red. Damn.

I yanked up her shirt and ran my fingers over her milky round cups. Moving my fingertips agonizingly slow over her perfect nipples. Her hot wetness was pooling out of her, soaking into her shorts and dampening my pants. Fuck yes. I sat up straight eyeing the cutie. "Strip" I said. Her cheeks turned pink, but she stood up, sliding off my lap she began removing her clothes. She shimmied out of her shorts, then removed her tank top. Her smooth skin glowed in the soft light of the room. Her sports bra cleverly hiding her swells, her underwear hugging her curvy hips. She glanced at me nervously, standing still. "All of it" I said. My body aching for more. Slowly she pulled her bra over her head. Her beautiful swells bouncing freely, she then slid her panties to the floor. Stepping out of them.

Now she stood in front of me, free of restraint. Beautiful. I licked my lips, feeling no better than the big bad wolf. "Sit" I said, pointing to my lap. She walked forward, and readied herself to straddle me, but I stopped her. "No no, beautiful. I want you turned around." Again, she blushed, but did as commanded. She turned her back to me and sat down. Her white ass snuggling into my lap.

Fuck, I want to bend her over. Lay her down and take her from behind. I gripped her hips as I ghosted my lips across her shoulder blades. "Mmm, I've been waiting for you. Antha, my sweet temptation." I nipped her shoulder, causing a squeak to jump from her chest. "Be a good girl and rock those hips for me baby" I said as I drifted one hand up her stomach brushing the tip of her nipple. She moved her hips, grinding against me as I began lightly pinching and pulling at her soft peaks. Mmm, sliding my other hand up her thigh, I tickled the hair on her mons. She froze, still so innocent. "Don't stop" I whispered into her ear. She, though hesitant, continued her rocking motion. Her nipple pressed firmly against my palm, rock hard.

With a smile, the fingertips of my free hand dipped into her warm folds. She was wet, her scent like an earthly cry bleeding desire, feeding my hunger. A low growl rumbled in my chest. "You're wet Antha, I think you might desire me. Is that true?" A moan trembled from her lips, along with a shaky 'yes'. I slid my fingers further down, encasing them inside her warmth. While lightly grazing her clit with my nails. She hissed; her hips jerked forward.

"What do you want me to do to you? This is kind of feeling a bit too sudden." She snorted a humorous laugh as she looked over her shoulder at me. "I want you to make me feel like you did the first time. No one else made me feel that way." Her eyes were dilated. Her voice serious. Huh, I don't know why but it really does make me happy to hear it. Maybe It's my ego. "I can do that, little girl" I huskily replied.

I locked my free arm around her, and smirked. She looked at me, somewhat confused. "The lady gets, what the lady wants." I said with a devilish smile. And proceeded to attack her clit. The rubs started out soft and gentle, getting progressively rougher and faster with each passing second. She silently cried out. Her hips jerking, her body shaking. I held on tighter to her. Rubbing her hard clit with no mercy. She was breathing heavy, repeating breathless I's with each exhale as I purposefully over stimulated her into delirium. She produced even more of her slick moisture, coating my fingers as she writhed on top of me. "Please, please!" I stood up keeping her upright. And walked her to what I hoped was her bedroom. She swayed, her legs weak. Perfect.

I pushed her down onto the bed, landing on her stomach. She was looking beautifully disheveled. Grabbing her hips, I lifted her backside up until she was on her knees. "Do you know what I'm going to do to you, little girl? I'm going to fuck you. I'm going to take you. And when I'm done, I'm going to turn you over, I'll strip down to nothing and sit on your stomach. Then I'm gonna finger myself until I have an orgasm. You will watch me, and you, you're going to like it." A guttural moan left her. Feeling my own arousal throbbing freely as I pushed my fingers into her. She was tight, holding my fingers in the prison of her bliss. I just held them in her for a few seconds. Her wet hotness clenched around me. I bit my bottom lip as I rubbed her smooth ass with my free hand. 'SMACK' giving her a not so light swat. She whimpered, now on her hands. Her creamy cheeks turning red. "Get ready Antha."

I pulled out of her just to the tip of my fingers. She was shaking. Her sweet opening trying to pull me back in. She was breathing heavy, gripping the bedsheets. I slammed into her. Passion took the wheel as I rocked my body into hers. So willing, so wanting. Her sweet moans and shocked gasps filled me to no end. Her hips rocking back into me. Begging for more. "Fuck! You're so tight. Naughty girl wants it rougher don't ya?" I asked, gripping her hip and slamming harder into her. "Yes!!" She cried out, rocking even faster. Pushing her shoulders down, her chest hit the bed. I held her down while slamming deeper.

"Oh God! Oh my God!" Smirking, my fingers curved, and she exploded. Arching her back, clawing the bed, and begging me to never stop. I pushed my fingers in harder. "I'm CUMMING!!" she screamed. I vaguely heard a door being opened but was too involved with Antha to care. I pushed my fingers deeper into her, sliding my leg between hers, and bending over her body. "You. Are. Mine!" and with each word I twitched my fingers within her, causing her to jump each time. Her heat rubbing against my thigh. Kissing her shoulders, I gently pulled out, then slowly back in. She hummed happily, sighing with contentment.

I rode out her orgasm. Letting her body climb down from its high. She pulsed around my fingers, clenching and relaxing as she tried to make the sensation stay as long as possible.

I pulled my fingers out of her, along with a gush of her womanly cum. I rolled her over, so that she was on her back. I want to ride her stomach, slide my wetness on her. Introduce her to my world of naughtiness. Bringing my fingers to my lips, I tasted her sweetness. Mmm, pure gold. Stepping back, I looked down at my work. Her body covered in a sheen of sweat, with a noticeable wet spot under her. An almost identical image of our first encounter. Her legs wide open, her hair wildly spread out on the bed, beautiful. Her fully robust chest raising and falling with each rapid breath. I want to please myself now, and I want those baby blues to watch me. But then I remembered the door, I looked behind me and saw a familiar face. Like the aged ghost of someone I once knew.

She had golden curls and green eyes. A birthmark on her left cheek... Wait a second.... Shit! Is that Tom's little sister? The same little sister that used to hang out with me? She used to hang onto my every word, always wanted to be where I was. Wanted to be my sister. But that all stopped when Sasha kicked me to the curb. It's been several years now. "Karen?" I asked, uncertain of my own memory. With wide eyes she looked at me then at Antha, then back to me.

"A-aunt Kelly?"

Fuck...

(.... To be continued....) ⊠

Chapter 18

# Jailbait

I know that it's wrong. I know this is bad. I know it, don't think I don't. But this girl does things to me. Things that I can hardly fight against. I'm old enough to be her mother. Yet I can't resist her. She has me bound. I am captured between her unmarked thighs, her curved hips, her soft voice, and naughty gaze. Though I tried, I couldn't resist her any longer. I couldn't stop myself; I didn't want to. And now her eyes are blindfolded, her hands are cuffed above her head, locked there by rope attached to a D-ring, her lips trembling, her body tense.

"Please Mistress, please." She whimpered quietly. Her skirt riding up by the gentle rocking of her hips. Not even the strongest of women could have resisted her, I doubt any of them would have wanted to. I looked down at her, her wanting body. Her pink tongue that licked at her lips. The need was clearly evident in her strained voice. She wants me to do things to her. She's begging for it. I don't know how she knew I was capable of such wicked and pleasurable crimes, but she did. And she pursued me. She pestered and teased. She'd call and text, she'd show up at my doorstep, in the pouring rain, begging for a chance... begging to be allowed to prove herself worthy.

I lightly trailed my fingers up her inner thigh. I could go to jail. I could be convicted. I could lose my job, my home, and my very mind. She'd get off free, with some counseling sessions about how the big bad female wolf tricked her. But little would they all know just how bad this sweet, innocent girl truly is. I may be a cougar, but she's a beautiful ally cat. Devious and deadly. How can someone so submissive be so powerful? How can someone so young, be so in charge? She's not normal... And in a sense, I guess, neither am I.

Her strong legs were clad in tights up to her mid-thigh, a simple plain dark gray skirt decorated her hips. She's so beautiful, a sinful angel here to drag me down. She wore an elegant white button up dress shirt, and a tie to match the skirt. Her lips red from her constant biting. I could own her. Turn her into my willing pet. I could tame her, possess her, make her feel empowered in serving me, make her mine... But I won't. She's young and has so much learning to do. It won't be my place to fully corrupt her. But I will taste her forbidden essence. I will feed upon her nectar and savor the taste soon gone from my lips. I will treasure this moment above many others...

I teased the edge of her tights; she was breathing heavy. Her chest rising and falling as her legs squeezed closed. She's been waiting patiently for this; constantly riding the vibration of the toy I placed between her legs. Rocking her hips against it while softly asking for more. She's so well behaved, even in her naughtiness. With a more aggressive touch, I gripped both her thighs and opened them wider. She fought against me, trying to hold them closed, but she gave in, a soft whimper leaving her lips. Her skirt lifted up a bit more, exposing her sexy red undies. A wet slit enticingly formed near her sweet opening. Damn... I could lose everything for Miss Innocent. And a part of me would. I'd give it up somewhat willingly... But I can't, it would ruin me. It would break us.

She doesn't know it. But this must be our last time. This has to be it, until she's older. But I'm going to enjoy it for a what it is right now. My forbidden little goddess. My sweet temptress. And I'm going to make sure she remembers this, that she won't forget me. I stepped between her legs, pulling her closer to the edge of the bed. Her shirt hiked up, revealing her smooth stomach. The heat of her crotch pressed against me. Exciting me to the core. But this is not for me, this is for her. I took ahold of her hips and yanked her closer. Effectively pushing the vibrator off of her. I grabbed it, holding it directly against her clit, through her underwear. She moaned, her hips rising up against me. I licked my lips and closed my eyes; letting her pleasure herself. Her sweet scent filling the room, her subtle innocence burning my restraint. For one last time, I will treasure the gift of her body, her beauty.

I held on tightly, in fear of this being my last chance to do so. I slowly slipped my hand up her thigh, letting the vibrator fall onto the bed. Brushing my fingertips against her damp kitten. She purred out, her hips slowing. Awaiting my demand, willing to take anything I choose to give her. But try as I might to think of a command to give, nothing comes. Nothing but the sad truth, and the even sadder reality. I pushed back those thoughts and watched her as she gently pulled against her restraints. Pulling closer to me. "You are so beautiful, my sweet girl." I pressed my fingers against her wetness, causing her hips to jerk up. "You vixen, you're my beautiful disaster. And you... You..." The words dried on my tongue. As the threat of tears dried my eyes. My beautiful tragedy, my willing demise. But I cannot speak that.

No more words. No more.

Instead, I slid the underwear off her, and bent over kissing her sweet lips deeply. Stealing her breath away, as she has stolen mine. I slid my hand between her smooth thighs, easing my fingers inside of her warm, wet lips. Just as I eased my tongue into her mouth. Without being asked, she began to suck. Causing my clit to throb for her. My hunger for her growing as she sucked the length of my tongue enthusiastically. A growl left me, warming my bones. Her young body moving sensually under me. Her teeth lightly grazed my tongue. I pressed two fingers against her opening, she clenched, her hips thrusting up for more. I closed my eyes. Then forced them open as I pushed into her. And with a hunger, I took her as if it were our last.

Thankful that she could not see the tears in my eyes. Or feel the pain in my chest. Her moans filled me, even as it broke me. The way she rocked, the force with which she squeezed around my fingers, calling out my name... I fell on top of her. Kissing her as if she were my air, and I, dying of suffocation. This girl has turned my world upside down... And I won't ever be the same.

Her essence gushed around my fingers, the faster I moved. Her legs spread wide for me. Her scent soaking into my sheets, my clothes, my soul. Mine, she will always be mine. "A piece of you will always belong to me little girl. Never forget that. I will hold onto it until my last days. But you will always know. I will always be your first. You. Are. Mine." I spoke with a thrust for each word. Causing her to bite her bottom lip and cling to me. Her legs locking me in place. "Mine!"

Her body arched as I sat up again, taking her with a passion. "Fuck, yes, yes Mistress! Fuck!" She moaned out. I grabbed her by her hair roughly with my free hand. "Watch your language, little girl." She whimpered, still riding my fingers.

"I love you Mistress!" She cried out. With a smile, I lifted her leg up, and continued slamming into her tight walls. She was writhing under me now. Shaking as she reached her release. Her hips came up off the bed as her body shook. Her clit pulsing under my thumb. I lightly stroked her stomach as she slowly lowered herself back to the bed, breathing heavy.

I slipped my fingers from inside of her, my eyes burning. I slid up next to her and unhooked her restraints. Then untied her blindfold. Beautiful brown eyes looked up at me. Clouded by a layer of lust and pleasure. I sweetly kissed her lips, as the haze lifted from her eyes. Immediately, concern filled her gaze. But before she could form a word of worry. I touched her full lips.

"You are so beautiful. And you have captured my heart, little one..." I touched her cheek. Gently caressing her. "This has to be our last time. We can't do this again." Her eyes widened; her bottom lip quickly began to tremble. "But why?" She whispered with a shaking in her voice. I smiled sadly at her. Then pulled her tightly against me. "Because the law will catch up with us. And the outcome will not be pretty." She hung unto my shirt tightly, already to tears. "Shhh" I soothed her, as I tried to sooth myself. "When you graduate, I want you to come find me. If you still want me... But this has to stop, my little vixen. I love you too much to continue this, like this. You deserve a love not in the shadows. You deserve something not hidden. And not forbidden."

"I want you" she spoke into my chest; her eyes shined with tears, as a smile spread on her lips. "I'll find you. I won't forget you. Promise..." She said, looking away. "You won't forget me...right? You won't find a different young girlfriend and forget about me?" I chuckled and kissed her forehead. “I couldn't even if I wanted to. You're the only young one I desire and crave. My sweet jailbait.”

☒

Chapter 19

# Snippet: Warden Me This

Nervous and shaking, I sat in the chair across from the Warden. Her hair was straight and brown, her almond shaped brown eyes watched me carefully. Her body clad in respectable army gear. She's definitely the warden for a reason. Even though she's beyond scary her eyes seemed soft. Her laugh lines just barely showed near her pink lips. Her hands were folded on the desk. I felt small, small in the eyes of a giant. I have no idea why I've been called up here. Regardless, here I am. "Angela." I inwardly cringed at my name. "Y-yes warden?" She smiled at me. She's a beautiful woman. Older than me by maybe 20 years. It's really hard to tell. "Well, I understand that you're new here." I nodded, fidgeting with my fingers. Staring down at my prison clothes, feeling sick. I've stayed so good for so long to end up here. Ha, it's so ironic that I can't even be outrageously upset about it. The truth is I was in the wrong place at the wrong time... And the wrong skin color during the wrong crime. So now, now I'm dead. Or close enough to it that it hurts a whole lot.

She sighed and leaned back. "The hell is a girl like you, doing in a place like this?... I know looks can be deceiving, but-" She looked down at a file on her desk. "It just doesn't make any plain sense... No criminal history, no tickets, not even a single house call. I don't get it." I smiled sadly at her. I know I could have said the ultimate thing to get off free. But to tell everyone my alter ego's identity would plunge my only source of income into a trickle.

"I was in the wrong place at the wrong time" I smiled again, meaning it more. "It's only for a year, and maybe when they re-question the guys, I'll be cleared." She nodded, seemingly unconvinced. "How'd you get Butch to start protecting you? She doesn't usually waste her time on newbies who can't protect themselves even a little. What are you doing for her?" I blushed and looked down, not sure how to answer. "Ahh, I see."

"NO!" I said, turning red. Her eyebrows went up. "It's not like that, I can't do much... I... I write." She smirked "You write?" I nodded looking up at her. She seemed amused. "Why the hell would she protect a writer?" I blushed even deeper, looking away. "I-it's what I write." She didn't speak, just waiting. I sighed. "I write lesbian erotica and she makes me write her something every few days in exchange for protection." She leaned back, watching me with a level of disbelief. "Okay, now tell me the real reason." I nervously twitched. "That's the real reason ma'am. Honest." She shook her head, a chuckle leaving her.

"Sorry if honesty doesn't go far here kid. You want me to believe that a sweet mild-mannered girl such as yourself could write the kind of erotica that Butch would like? Excuse me if it seems hard to believe." I smiled nervously. "There's nothing more I can say about it Warden ma'am. It's all I know how to do, it's simply what I am." Her steady eyes watched me. "Prove it" my head snapped up, cheeks already burning.

"Ma'am?" I asked, uncertain as to where this was going. "Prove it. I want to see this for myself. I want to see the next finished product on my desk, then I'll decide if I believe you."

## Chapter 20, Bonus Chapter

# Hate

There's no other word for how I feel about her. She's an aggravating, arrogant, and stupid know it all! She's always right! And so freaking perfect. Forget her! I stormed out of the classroom with burning cheeks of humiliation. I just can't... no, I can believe that she's that evil. I've been saying it for years. She's the devil. I'm sure of it. She doesn't have one pure bone in her whole freaking body! She has no moral compass and doesn't care about anything but herself. She's a selfish prick and I'm not sure she's ever said a kind word in her entire freaking life!

I grumbled all the way to my locker and yanked it open. Ignorant, self-absorbed, conceited, conniving! I slammed the locker, ready to punch it when someone grabbed my arm. I jumped and turned around, two heart beats away from breaking my 'No freak outs at school' rule. Only to see that I now stood face to face with the devil herself. Her dark eyes were lowered, with an easy smirk permanently pressed on her perfect red lips. She was taller than me by far, a lot stronger too. But I'm no welcome mat, and she's been pushing my buttons since day one! I squared my shoulders and I sized her up. Not letting my stance waver, she wants a fight then let's go! Because I'm seriously getting tired of her. I've done nothing to her! Yet she always has to correct me, always upstage me! Always makes me feel insignificant and small. Well dang it, just because I don't do bad things, and I don't curse... It doesn't mean I'm a brown noser or holier-than-thou. I just... I just... I fought back the wave of tears that threatened to slip out.

Who am I kidding? I'm weak. I'm not a fighter. And I know I can be a teacher's pet by some standards. It's not that I'm trying to get on the teacher's good side. I truly do value the teachers input and opinions, and I want to learn, in fact I love learning. I came from a broken home and having an education is the only way out. I just want peace, but she challenges me at every step! Every time, every corner, of every day!

"What do you want Da'ville?" I sneered at her. She always seems to bring out the worst in me. And I'm getting more than my fair share of aggravation. Standing up straight, she smiled at me as if coming to some type of solid conclusion. And that smile scares me. Evil only smiles when it's won. Fear gripped my insides as I took a quick glance of my surrounding, only to find the halls unusually empty. I was alone... with her. And stuck between her and my locker. Just great. I'm dead.

"Let's make a deal" she said with a sly grin. I glared at her. A deal? Who does she think she is, Howie Mandel? But again, I honestly can't fight, I also don't have a great love for pain... So maybe it's worth listening to? Without speaking for fear of saying the wrong thing, I nodded my willingness to at least listen to her speak, and kept my trap shut.

"Okay Princess, the deal is this, if you let me have just one kiss..." She held up a single digit, with a sly smile. "One solid kiss on the lips. And if you don't like it, then I'll leave you alone, I won't bother you in class, I won't talk to you when you want nothing to do with me. Hell, I'll even pretend that you're invisible. I won't pick the same projects as you, and if we're forced to be partners, I'll either request a different one, or let you take the lead on the assignments..."

This sounds too good to be true...

"However, if you do like it... Well, I guess the fun has only just begun... Deal or no deal?" This time I was the one who smirked. Of course I won't like it, duh she's a girl, I'm a girl. Genetically and religiously speaking, I won't like it at all! It's kinda a lose win for me, but yay! She'll leave me alone. Then I can finish out my school days in peace. No more of her arrogance, no more of her chuckling, no more of her constant teasing... No more of her dark eyes baring into my soul from across the room. No more of her voice sneaking into my brain and mixing up all my thoughts. No more of her soft whispers when no one is looking. No more of her grungy compliments that make me turn red and run away. No more of her constant smirks, and boastful laugh... Ahh, life is going to be good... I think. Why am I questioning this?... Of course, it will be!

Honestly! The only downside being that I have to kiss her. I can do this, it's for the betterment of my education. With a big smile, I spoke "I've said it once and I'll say it again, you're evil Ezmer. Your daddy must be Satan and your mama a witch, because you've got an ungodly soul..." Her eyes flared in anger. As she took a threatening step towards me. "...b-but, if a kiss is all it takes... Th-then I'll do it."

Before the words were completely passed my lips, in a flash almost too fast to be normal, she had my back pressed against my locker. Her hand fisted into my thick black hair, pulling my head back. Forcing me to look up at her. Into those dark, mysterious eyes. They held me, as they have done so many times, exposing hidden truths within my soul. I felt so insignificantly small, yet oddly large. Because this time, I know I'll win this one. I'll finally have one up on her. It's as good as golden.

But... the way she looked down at me, her dark eyes dilated and glaring into my soul, made my heart beat a little faster. My breath quickened, and she had me seeing double. She has this ability about her, this mystic air that is unsettling, as well as fascinating. And I can't help but to be drawn to it. But at the same time, completely repulsed by it.

"Deal" she growled, in what almost sounded like it came out of a wild animal. Then she slammed her mouth into mine. To my surprise, it was far more than the peck on the lips I was expecting. No, this was a full-on assault, and it knocked the air from my lungs. Her hot, soft lips worked mine with skill, drowning me in emotions I never knew existed. Her lips forced mine to open. Her tongue, as lithe and smooth as a snake, slipped passed my lips. Causing my entire body shiver. A gasp shook from me, and my knees felt weak. What is this? Is this lust? This can't be lust! She's a girl!

But even as I thought those evasive thoughts, she was pushing me harder against the locker. Her free hand ran up my side, causing goosebumps to decorate my already flushed skin. Whatever this is, it's pulling me in. And without my say, my lips kissed just as hard, I couldn't tell them to stop. My tongue played just as rough; it wouldn't quit! I can't breathe right; I was gasping for air yet not caring if I suffocated. Down, in my forbidden place, between my thighs, a burning sensation was being born. One I've never known... Yet at the same time, I don't want it to leave. The way she kissed me, made me want it more. How she touched me, begged me to crave it. The burning thing grew like an unstoppable wildfire and was causing something hot to bubble inside of me.

Something tight, something deep, something naughty. For the first time in my life, I was wanting and craving the things everyone said was bad. Her hand rested outside my place, in front of my fire. Her fingers wiggling, pressing harder against the crotch of my pants. My heart slammed into my chest, almost painfully. I felt lightheaded, my hands fisted at my side, I don't think I've taken a single breath this whole time. And almost too soon she pulled away from me. Both of us were breathing heavy, her dark eyes looked at me with a deep fire in them. Like the pits of hell ablaze with passion. The flames danced around her pupils, trapping me in their grasp. Her lips were swollen, and even redder than normal, her cheeks flushed. Her pink tongue peeked out and licked her lips, moistening them with the shiny tip. My eyes followed the moment, I was completely transfixed on her... And confused. I... I wasn't supposed to like it... I wasn't supposed to like it!

She smirked at me, then leaned in close. My whole body was shaking, wanting, waiting for more. Her lips brushed my cheek as her warm breath fanned my ear in a way that opened my innocent eyes to the most forbidden of all fruit. And in a voice so husky it screamed lust and fear she whispered. "Never, make a deal with the devil."

Alter Egos Publishing greatly acknowledges Kindle Direct Publishing for the support and opportunities.

Book and cover design by Faye Love

Edited by: Mickeythered

Published by: Alter Egos Publishing

Publisher's Website: Alteregospublishing.com

Cover photography: Malov Sergii Sergeevich

Photographer's website: Serega.com.ua

Printed in Great Britain
by Amazon

43252832R00057